Meow.

I looked down when I felt the orange tab¹ ···il
drag along my shin.

"Hey, kitty." I bent down and put ···
kitty, kitty."

It was the closest the cat ha'···

"Wee-doggie, it's hot in ' ··· ···rn up."
Granny scurried through the fr··· ···neral home.
"Not as hot as the cleavage of M··· ···boobs, but still
hot."

She dragged off her big purple sunglasses and focused
her eyes on me. She glared at me like I'd better straighten
up or she was going to jerk a knot in me.

"Granny." I stood up and put my arms out to walk over
to give her a hug.

Her spiky red-haired head twisted right, left, and
around before she jerked her five-feet-four-inch frame back
over to me. She smacked her palm on my forehead.

"You got the trauma?" She gave me the wonky eye.

"No." I took a step back. "I'm fine."

"You were looking awfully strange when I walked
into the door with your hand out. You might not've thought
I heard you, but I heard you call for a kitty." Granny
pointed into the viewing room. "There's no kitty in there,
just Shelley Shaw who's going to melt if you don't get
something done about this humidity."

"Here Mr. Whiskers. Here kitty." The ghost of the
young girl that had come on the day of Charlotte Rae's
funeral reappeared out of nowhere. She twirled her pigtail
around her finger. "Remember me? You said you'd help
me cross over."

STRUNG OUT TO DIE
CRIMPED TO DEATH

A Ghostly Southern Mystery Series
A GHOSTLY UNDERTAKING
A GHOSTLY GRAVE
A GHOSTLY DEMISE
A GHOSTLY MURDER
A GHOSTLY REUNION
A GHOSTLY MORTALITY
A GHOSTLY SECRET

Kenni Lowry Mystery Series
FIXIN' TO DIE
SOUTHERN FRIED
AX TO GRIND
SIX FEET UNDER

TONYA

KAPPES

A

GHOSLTY

SECRET

A GHOSTLY SOUTHERN MYSTERY

Book Seven

TONYA KAPPES

Tonyakappes.com

Copyright

This book is a work of fiction. The characters, incidents, and dialogue are drawn from the author's imagination and are not to be construed as real. Any resemblance to actual events or persons, living or dead, is entirely coincidental.

Acknowledgements

Writing a book is a lonely journey, but I'm so fortunate to have so many wonderful people in my life that integral to the writing process. Cyndy Ranzau is a lifeline and amazing editor. Without her, my stories wouldn't nearly make as much sense.

And the covers! They bring so much of the book to visual life. Jessica Fischer is amazing and has done that with each book.

Then Eddy. The love of my life. Without his constant encouragement and dedication to the writing process as much as I am, I'm not sure I could've done this without him.

Of course…The Cozy Krew!!! Truly, you guys rock. You keep me motivated and inspired.

Xoxo ~Tonya

Chapter One

Ghosts sure are a funny thing. The afterlife was something I didn't think I'd ever figure out. Even as a Betweener and after helping at least seven ghosts cross over to the other side, I still didn't understand them.

My latest Betweener client sat near the casket in the front of the viewing room with a book in her lap. She'd been hanging around for about six months now with little to no advancement on her case.

"She sure could charm the dew right off the honeysuckle." Mary Anna Hardy stood over the mahogany wood high-gloss casket with the white velvet interior looking at her handiwork, and took my stare away from the little ghost. "Damn shame she drank herself silly."

"Damn," the ghost girl repeated. I'd found that my young client loved to repeat dirty words. "What?" she asked when she noticed me raise my brows toward her. She stuck the end of one of her pigtails in her mouth and chewed on it.

"Seeing that she died from liver failure that was due to drinking, I'd bet Eternal Slumber that half of her charm was due to the fact she was always sweet talking to get another free drink. At least that's what I'd heard she did down at The Watering Hole," John Howard Lloyd, maintenance man of Eternal Slumber, took the Swiffer mop and ran it over the walls to get any dust off.

It was a handy trick and he was tall enough to run it from ceiling to floor, not like me. I'd had to get a stepladder just to reach the top of the window casing.

Granted, all the windows in Eternal Slumber, my funeral home business, were practically floor to ceiling with big wooden casing around them. After all, the funeral home was located in a very old Victorian house that'd been converted into the funeral home that my family had owned. Now it was mine. All mine.

I sighed deeply thinking about the last six months as my eyes gazed up at Mary Anna and John Howard and back to the little ghost. Shelley Shaw had been found in the gravel right outside of The Watering Hole. According to Jack Henry Ross, my boyfriend and local sheriff, Shelley hadn't even been in the bar. Apparently, she died of her own doing according to her autopsy and I wouldn't be seeing her ghost. It was always hard to have a funeral for someone so young.

The last person that young was my sister, Charlotte Rae. Truly it's taken me the last six months to start feeling somewhat normal. Even Zula Fae Raines Payne, my granny, had just begun to show her spry self again.

"You sure do pretty work," John Lloyd said to Mary Anna, referring to the cosmetology work she'd done on Shelley.

"It's an art." She had a pair of scissors in her hand. Her wrist twirled around as she talked; the sharp end pointed out made John Howard duck each time the twirl circled back to him. "A gift, really."

She reached over the casket and did a few final snips of Shelley's hair. John Howard went on about the rest of his work. The florist had delivered the flowers and had set them in the foyer. With a couple of the baskets in each hand, I walked back into the viewing room and set them on some of the floating shelves on the wall. After the last basket was in place, the casket spray was the last one and prettiest one. It was from Shelley's family and done up in red roses. The gold banner across the blanket of flowers read: BELOVED.

I stood in the back of the viewing room to make sure that it looked aesthetically pleasing. Rows of folding chairs were set up with one aisle down the middle. The red slipcovers with the Eternal Slumber logo embroidered on the back were neatly tied on the chairs. I walked around to all the windows and fluffed out the baby blue floor-to-ceiling drapes.

"Emma Lee," Mary Anna called me and turned around. The red lipstick almost took away from her white Daisy-Duke shorts and red-and-white gingham button down that was tied in a knot at her bellybutton. "I'm done. I've got to get back down to the shop." She unbuttoned the first four buttons of her shirt and let the girls bust out. "Business is slow." She stuck her hand in her bra and shimmied them things up to her chin. "I've got to call in backup."

I laughed and waved 'bye, shaking my head with each twist of her hips. I could only imagine what she looked like walking down the sidewalk to Girl's Best Friend Spa, the only salon in Sleepy Hollow, Kentucky, our little slice of heaven among the caves and caverns.

I ran my hand down my brown hair. It was time I get a highlight and a new cut. It was time I did a lot of things, like come back to the living. A little piece of me died with Charlotte Rae. Yeah. Like every sibling, Charlotte Rae and I had our fair share of disagreements. We never saw things the same way and at the very end it was a shame because it was only then that she truly knew who I really was.

Today wasn't the day to get sad or depressed. The visitor log had to be put out on the stand and the memorial cards needed to be stacked.

Meow.

I looked down when I felt the orange tabby cat's tail drag along my shin.

"Hey, kitty." I bent down and put my hand out. "Here kitty, kitty."

It was the closest the cat had ever gotten to me.

"Wee-doggie, it's hot in here. Ah'm bout to burn up." Granny scurried through the front door of the funeral home. "Not as hot as the cleavage of Mary Anna's boobs, but still hot."

She dragged off her big purple sunglasses and focused her eyes on me. She glared at me like I'd better straighten up or she was going to jerk a knot in me.

"Granny." I stood up and put my arms out to walk over to give her a hug.

She completely bypassed me and looked into the viewing room. Her spiky red-haired head twisted right, left, and around before she jerked her five-feet-four-inch frame back over to me. She smacked her palm on my forehead.

"You got the trauma?" She gave me the wonky eye.

"No." I took a step back. "I'm fine." I crossed my heart.

Technically I didn't lie. I didn't have what Doc Clyde called the Funeral Trauma. Two years ago this Christmas, I had walked down to Artie's Meat and Deli to get me and Charlotte Rae a soup and sandwich for lunch. All the Christmas decorations were up and Artie had put a plastic Santa on the roof of the deli. It was particularly warm for a December day in Kentucky, which helped melt the snow. As soon as I walked up to the deli, the Santa fell off the roof and knocked me out cold. When I woke up a few days later in the hospital, I was surrounded by family and clients. Let me clarify, the clients were dead ones. Ones I'd put six feet into the ground, only they'd not crossed over.

I'd mentioned to Doc Clyde that I could see them and he claimed I had what was called the Funeral Trauma and I'd been around dead people too long. In reality, Santa had given me a gift not on my list. The title of Betweener, the gift of seeing dead people. Really dead murdered people that needed me to help bring their killer to justice. Fast forward a couple of years to now and I've still got Betweener clients. The cat was my first animal client and it'd been around for at least a year now.

The chime of the old grandfather clock that sat in the corner of the foyer chimed. There were only thirty minutes until show time.

"You were looking awfully strange when I walked into the door with your hand out. You might not've thought I heard you, but I heard you call for a kitty." Granny pointed into the viewing room. "There's no kitty in there, just Shelley Shaw who's going to melt if you don't get something done about this humidity."

"Here Mr. Whiskers. Here kitty." The ghost of the young girl that had come on the day of Charlotte Rae's funeral reappeared out of nowhere. She twirled her pigtail around her finger. "Remember me? You said you'd help me cross over."

Chapter Two

"I don't understand why you don't talk to me," the ghost rotated her body back and forth. Her little blue eyes stared up at me and she clutched a book to her chest. "Did I do something wrong?"

A few of the Auxiliary women were standing at the entrance of the viewing room waiting to sign the guest book. I offered them a wry smile that was part thank you for coming and part sympathy. It was hard. I had to be seen as someone who felt their pain as well as put on a good social event.

Yes. As sick as it sounded, funerals in Sleepy Hollow were just as much a social gathering as a birth, wedding, birthday, or any hoedown. I'd guess that half of the people sitting in the chairs in the viewing room hadn't ever talked to Shelley Shaw a day in their life.

I stepped aside and headed down the hall toward the back of Eternal Slumber. On the right were two offices, one was mine, and the other had been Charlotte's. The elevator went to the basement where Vernon Baxter, my undertaker who was also the county coroner, worked. The basement also served as the county morgue.

The morgue might give someone the heebie-jeebies, but it was actually a state-of-the-art facility with all the bells and whistles. It was a genius idea really. After Vernon was elected coroner of Sleepy Hollow, since it didn't require full-time work, he kept his day job here at Eternal Slumber. The old morgue was run down and was like one of those creepy made for TV movie kinds. Even had the flickering lights. I'd gone to the town council and proposed that they could use my facility, in turn, any equipment purchased to upgrade the county morgue would also be available to be used by Eternal Slumber. Surprisingly they agreed and voted yes. Vernon was hunky-dory in that basement.

Also down the hall was a small gathering room where the family members could go and have a timeout from all the mourners. There was food back there from the Auxiliary women. Funerals were their time to shine and try to outdo one another with their recipes.

But I was headed to my little apartment in the back of the old Victorian. I'd grown up in the funeral home. Trust me, no one ever wants to spend the night in a funeral home, so as a young girl, I wasn't the most popular kid in school. I'd say I was the least popular. After my parents retired, I brought the funeral home up-to-date by adding new fixtures, new paint, new drapes and added another viewing room. I did keep a small apartment in the back that had an efficiency kitchen, small TV room, bathroom and a bedroom. There was even my own entrance.

I'm not going to say it's not creepy sleeping in the same building with cold bodies, but nothing fazed me now that I could see ghosts.

I shut the door to my apartment and locked it so Granny couldn't just walk in, even though she did have a key. At least I could hear her fussing under her breath and jiggling her key, giving me time to stop talking to the little girl. Trust me, if Granny caught me talking to myself, she'd have Doc Clyde over here in no time flat.

"I'm not ignoring you." I bent down to the little girl. "Every time I ask you to give me some information, you can't." I sighed. It was times like right now that I wished I could reach out and touch my clients. "I really do wish I could help you."

"But you ignore me." Her little voice cracked.

"Here's the deal. Those people out there." I pointed toward the front of the funeral home. "They don't know I can see you. If they see me talking to myself, they will think I'm crazy and call a doctor to tell him I'm not feeling well."

"You gonna get a shot?" She shivered. "I hate shots." She rubbed her arm like she had a memory.

"You remember getting shots?" I asked trying to coax her to talk to me.

When she showed up on the day of my sister's funeral, she was with another woman she claimed was her sister. They fought like they were sisters, but then the sister was gone. I realized it was a ghost even though she told me she was a Betweener like me. She wasn't. It just goes to show you can't trust ghosts.

"Mr. Whiskers!" The little girl's attention swiftly turned to the cat when he appeared. She was able to pet on him and rub him. All I could do was feel his tail when he'd rub it against me.

"You still can't remember if Mr. Whiskers was your cat?" I asked, like I'd done several times.

She shook her head and giggled when Mr. Whiskers licked her fingers. The knock at the door that led into the funeral home startled her and the cat. They disappeared.

"Coming," I called and ran my hand down my black suit jacket. I wore the same thing to each funeral. Black pantsuit. I swung the door open and Jack Henry Ross stood on the other side.

"Hi," his whisper swept past my ears as did the smell of his cologne.

My stomach tumbled and rolled. I wanted to sop him up like gravy with a biscuit, but the time and place wasn't now or here.

"Why are you hiding back here?" He eyed me suspiciously.

"You look so hot." I referred to his blue uniform he always wore for the funeral processions. Even though he was sheriff, out of respect for the families and our small town, he always led the cars from Eternal Slumber to the cemetery.

He winked, pulling me to him for a nice long kiss.

"Now spill." He lowered his eyes. "Ghost girl? Ghost cat?"

"Yeah. She was upset that I ignore her when people are around." I flip-flopped my head shoulder to shoulder. "There's not much I can do if she can't tell me more than her age. I don't know where she's from. I've scoured all the missing persons and hospitals over the last months and no one that looks like her has been reported missing or dead."

Granted, ghosts didn't look exactly as vibrant as they did when they were living. It was only when they were about to cross over that I could see how they had truly looked. It was probably good too because it left me with a good image of them instead of the muted ghost spirit that I was used to seeing.

"After the cemetery I've got a reservation for supper at Bella Vino Restorante and an appointment with Debbie Dually," he said and squeezed my hand.

"What on earth did I do to get supper and Debbie?" I gulped.

Before Charlotte crossed over, she was visiting me while I was in the hospital. I'd moved Jack's coat and a velvet ring box had fallen out of his jacket. Now. . .in high school I'd cut his pictures out of the yearbook and pasted them on my wall. Many nights I dreamed of marrying him, but right now wasn't the time for me to get engaged. It wasn't that I didn't see myself with him, heck, I already had my wedding dress picked out as well as all the colors, cake, food, venue and music. It was just my heart wasn't in the right place. Even though Charlotte told me that she'd be with me in spirit when I got married and I had to do it without her, I wasn't ready. Not now. Not yet.

"Why don't we just go see Debbie?" I suggested.

Debbie Dually was the medium who told me exactly the name of my gift. Betweener. She'd helped out so much and I needed her now. I'd never had a ghost I didn't know or a little girl. The thought of someone killing her really did bug me and I just didn't know how I was going to proceed. Maybe I was blocked or something.

"No. We've got something to celebrate." His slow southern drawl still sent my heart into a rapid beating fit. His deep brown eyes stared at me, making me want to reach out and run my fingers through his brown hair that had grown out a little from the high and tight he normally sported.

"Oh." I gnawed on my bottom lip wondering how I was going to get out of this one. I just knew he was taking me to our favorite restaurant to propose. I bit back the tears. The thought of me getting married without Charlotte Rae was really heavy on my heart. "Okay," I whispered and put it in the back of my head.

I'd do something, but right now I had to get back to Shelley Shaw's funeral.

Chapter Three

"Sh...sh...shell," the little girl sat on the top of Shelley's casket trying to sound out the sash on the casket spray while Julie Miller's gospel, *All My Tears*, played over the loud speaker.

I couldn't help but think if Shelley Shaw knew her time was coming to an end since she'd had this song playing in her car the night they found her body.

And I will not be ashamed. For my Savior knows my name. It don't matter where you bury me. I'll be home and I'll be free, Julie belted out and made me wonder if Shelley sang these words and had wished to be free from the grip alcohol had seemed to have on her.

"Let's pray." Pastor Brown's razor-sharp blue eyes scanned the crowd to make sure everyone's head was bowed and eyes were clamped tight. If they weren't he'd curse you with those eyes until the fear of God was in you, which made you close your eyes.

He put his hands up in the air. The sleeve on his already too short brown pinstriped suit coat exposed a tarnished metal watch. His pale skin stood out against his coal-black greasy comb-over.

"He sure is scary lookin'." The little girl appeared next to Pastor Brown and looked up at him with a snarl on her face. "Are you sure he's not a ghost like me? He's awfully white."

Granny nudged me when I giggled.

"Act like you got some sense," she warned with a whisper but her whisper was as loud as a train whistle.

"What's wrong with you, laughing while someone is lying corpse?" She bent down and scratched her legs to high-heaven.

Pastor Brown's voice boomed as he cracked one eye open and mentally told me to hush.

I rolled my lips together and looked down. Mr. Whiskers was dancing between Granny's ankles.

"I'm so itchy." She gave one last scratch before she gave up, giving me the head nod to follow her. "You got any itch cream?"

"Not a bit." Even though we were in the foyer, I kept my voice down.

"I've got some at the Inn." She grabbed my hand and dragged me out of the funeral home and down the steps.

The square, what we locals called the downtown area of Sleepy Hollow, was just that, a square with businesses on the circumference, like shops, local business, the courthouse and The Sleepy Hollow Inn. In the center was a big park with a large gazebo in the middle where people tended to gather.

Granny stalked across the street, through the park, and across the street again to The Sleepy Hollow Inn, or as locals called it the Inn, where she was the proud proprietor.

"Don't it look good?" Granny stood in the front yard of the Sleepy Hollow Inn with her hands on her hips as she looked at the freshly painted inn. After about a second, she started to itch again.

"It does look good." The pale yellow had been freshened up to more of a lemon yellow. With time it'd fade like before. There was a long porch along the front with four white pillars.

The white rocking chairs were occupied by guests of the Inn.

"Good night for a funeral, ain't it?" Granny greeted the guests in only a way she could. The guests looked half-scared, half-amused. "Get on in here before you let the bugs in." Granny held the screened door for me.

The inside of the Inn was very homey and inviting. It was the only place to stay within downtown Sleepy Hollow, so it was always filled. There were many returning guests because they love Granny's down-home hospitality. Though I think they liked her blunt attitude which some could mistake as crazy.

The big room on the right was the hospitality room where Granny kept refreshments for her guests. Most of the guests were in town to explore the caves and caverns. Some would even camp, but keep their room at the Inn. The room to the right was a dining room that was also open to the public. That's where everyone experienced Granny's southern cooking. Up the stairs were the guest rooms. Granny also lived there so it was hard for her too to separate work from life.

While Granny walked to the kitchen, I walked into the refreshment room and grabbed a couple of her chocolate chip cookies and a glass of sweet tea. Granny made the best sweet tea in the entire state of Kentucky and I'd bet the funeral home on it.

"What are you doing in here?" She came back in with a tube of itch cream. She unscrewed the top and squeezed out a glob. She bent over and smacked the goop on each ankle. "Darn fleas. You've got fleas in the funeral home. Get an exterminator."

"I'm sure I don't have fleas." I watched as the red bumps got bigger on her ankles.

"I'm telling you that I've not had a reaction like this since I was a kid and took home a cat with fleas. I'm allergic to cats and to fleas. You ain't got no cat, so I'm telling you it's fleas." She snarled. "So what's going on with you? How have you been, kiddo?"

She grabbed a glass and poured some tea, gesturing me to follow her back out to the front porch.

"You know. It's still not getting any easier." I referred to the loss of Charlotte. "I think it's going to take time."

"Time is flying by. You might need to go see a doctor." She cocked a brow and started to give the ferns a drink of her sweet tea by pouring some in each pot. She claimed it was magic food for them.

They were gorgeous and bouncy and perfect for the start of fall. Maybe if I drank more of Granny's tea, I'd be gorgeous and bouncy. I sighed.

"And I think Jack Henry wants to propose." It came out of my mouth like a bad thing.

"You sound like it's a death sentence." She picked and plucked the ferns to get out some of the soon-to-be-dead pieces. "I sure do remember you swooning all over that boy when you were a teenager. Ain't it just like a woman to get what she wants and don't want it?"

"Oh. I do love him." There was no denying that. "I never imagined myself getting married without Charlotte Rae and for some reason I feel like my happiness doesn't feel appropriate."

"If I recall, and don't go thinking I got memory loss because I don't, but if I do recall, Charlotte Rae did tell you to go and be happy according to your dream." Her eyes narrowed and she brought the glass up to her lips and let the last little drops of tea fall into her mouth.

The last time I spoke to Charlotte Rae's ghost played in my head like a movie.

"No." I gulped back the bittersweet moment. "Not without you by my side."

"I have to." Charlotte ghosted herself next to my bed. *"I'm sorry for not being the big sister you wanted me to be. You are going to be a beautiful bride."*

She pointed to the coat.

"Now pick it up and act like you don't know anything about it." She looked so angelic with the brightest smile across her face. Her eyes lit up like stars. *"Let him wow you with how much he loves you and adores you."*

After that I'd told Granny that I'd had a dream about Charlotte Rae. I couldn't tell her the truth about my Betweener gig.

"I'm telling you that spirits come to us in our dreams and she wants you to get married to Jack Henry as much as I do." Her eyes slid past me, across the town square, and over to Eternal Slumber where John Howard was getting the hearse ready for the drive to the cemetery.

Jack Henry stood on the front porch of the funeral home and waved me over.

"Look at that boy," Granny said in her saucy voice. "Now, you get on over there, finish up Shelley Shaw and get a ring on that finger. Good gawd, you're gonna be a thirty-year-old maid in a few days."

I grumbled the entire way over to the funeral home. It was true. I was going to be thirty in a few days and had hoped she'd forgotten since Charlotte was always on the forefront of our minds.

"It's gonna be your birfday?" The little girl appeared. I couldn't help but smile at her lisp. "I loved mine. I think I'm eight."

"You're eight?" I asked with my eyes still on the funeral home as I walked across the square. My shoulders dropped when I noticed she'd disappeared. It was the first real fact that she might've told me about since she showed up.

Chapter Four

"I wish so bad that you could see Mr. Whiskers." I was bent over in the passenger seat of Jack Henry's police cruiser laughing about the cat teasing Granny on our way out of Sleepy Hollow.

It was so much nicer than driving my car. . .the hearse.

"Granny was fit to be tied. She hates cats so I knew Mr. Whiskers was doing it to bug her." I shook my head and looked out the window.

The forty-minute drive to Lexington from Sleepy Hollow was beautiful. Especially this time of the year when the summer leaves were losing their vibrant green coat and turning into yellows, oranges, and a few reds. The Kentucky bluegrass was still lush as we drove the two-lane curvy country road that was lined with one horse farm after the other.

"It was a nice funeral. I did feel sorry for the family." He reached over with one hand and patted my leg. "You always make the services so nice."

"Thank you," I whispered and looked out the window. "I'm really excited you got an appointment with Debbie. I was thinking about doing it, but you know how much I try to keep my secret close to the vest."

"With Doc and Granny always looking at you, I can see why." He gave me a saucy wink and squeeze of the leg sending my heart right down to the tips of my toes. "I'll take care you."

Oh the times I'd prayed to hear those words.

"Are you sure this ghost is the only thing bothering you?" he asked after there were a few minutes of silence.

"It's the fact that she's a little girl. What do you think her parents are thinking?" I asked, tears forming in my eyes. "I'm lucky I've got this gift. I can truly help people. If I find out who she is, I can tell her parents."

"Whoa." Jack Henry was trying to reel me in. "You know that people can't know you see the ghosts of murdered people. If Debbie can help you and you do get some leads, we will do what we always do."

The comfort of knowing I wasn't alone was nice. When I had my first Betweener client and before Jack Henry and I even had our first date, he could tell I knew something about Ruthie Sue Payne. It looked like she'd tripped down the Sleepy Hollow Inn stairs and died, but she was pushed. She told me. I encouraged Jack Henry to investigate but when Granny was his number one suspect, I had to tell him that I could see Ruthie's ghost. What was even more magical. . .he believed me! We pretended to go on dates but we had teamed up. I'd give him clues Ruthie would give me about her death and he'd investigate.

In most cases, my clients didn't see who killed them. And in the afterlife, everyone loved them and didn't have a bad word to say.

"We are a team." I looked at the small brick house. Debbie and her young son, David, sat on the front porch.

Debbie waved. She had on a pair of blue jeans and a black tank top. She stood all of five feet tall, with a short brown bob with blunt bangs, hitting right at her eyebrows.

"Hi, Emma and Jack!" David smiled.

"Your tooth grew in." I smiled back at the precious little boy who'd had a big gap in his teeth the last time I was here.

"Yes, ma'am." He stuck his finger in his mouth, using the pad of his finger to wiggle another loose one back and forth. "Soon."

"David," Debbie put her hand on his shoulder. "Why don't you get inside and finish up your school project."

"Yes, Mama." He scurried inside.

Debbie caught the door before it slammed and she opened it.

"Please come in." We stepped inside. "You too," she said out the door. "Come on, honey. It's okay."

The little ghost girl came in with the book hugged up to her chest, looking somewhat timid.

"Can you see me?" she asked Debbie. Debbie nodded. "The last lady that said she could see me was a ghost. She even told me she was my sister. I always wanted a sister."

"She doesn't have a sister." My eyes popped open. "This was the first bit of information she's given me."

"You know how this works." Debbie pointed into the dining room where her glass top table was filled with lit candles and a burning incense. She picked up the incense with one hand and a feather in the other. She walked around the room brushing the feather in the smoke.

It was her way of cleansing the area free of spirits other than the little girl's. Jack and I sat down. The little girl was fascinated by Debbie. She didn't take her eyes off of Debbie. She giggled when Debbie took the feather and brushed it along her nose.

"Ghosts don't remember everything. Just bits and pieces. Little ones really don't have a lot of memory. Oh." Debbie smiled. "A cat. You have a cat."

Mr. Whiskers had ghosted up on the table. The little girl put her hands to her side. One still gripped the book, but she was a little more relaxed.

"We know that her demise was not an acceptable form since she's visiting you." Debbie sat down in the chair across from us. "And I think that Mr. Whiskers and she died together."

"My name is Betsy Lynn. What's yours?" she asked Debbie.

"Betsy Lynn," I whispered. "Her name is Betsy."

"I'm Debbie. A friend of Emma's, but I can't help you. That's Emma's job. I'm here to help ask some questions so she can help you and Mr. Whiskers."

"Can you tell me about the woman that was with her six months ago?" I asked.

"Oh, yes. Those sneaky ghosts. They are just wandering spirits. Most of the time they attach to children ghosts. They get the little ones to trust them and follow them, but when they came across you, Betsy here is too smart to fall for her tricks once she saw that you could really help her. Isn't that right, Betsy?" Debbie asked.

"Yes. My daddy used to say I was smart. I liked school and reading. I love to read." She bounced on her toes. This was the most excited I'd seen her.

"She loves the library. Go to the library." Debbie started to give me some information on where to start. "Type in Betsy and missing children into the database."

"Do you think it was an abduction?" I asked.

Debbie closed her eyes. Her face grew serious. Her jaw would tense and release and tense. Her head bobbled.

"She knew the person. I can't see who the person is. But I do see Betsy taking the hand and walking to a barn. The barn is dark. Betsy is scared. There's a barn cat. He's comforting Betsy." A tear trickled down Debbie's face. "She's so scared."

"Thank you," I whispered as the rims of my eyes became wet.

Jack Henry scooted his chair over and put his arm around me. There was nothing better than his warm embrace.

"I feel you." Debbie's eyes opened and she looked at me. "Your heart hurts." She looked between Jack Henry and me like she could see right inside of me. "You must let go of Charlotte Rae and move forward in your life. That was Charlotte's last wish," she reminded me.

Jack rubbed his hand up and down my back as the tears fell like a waterfall down my cheeks. Debbie pushed a box of Kleenex across the table.

"You have to focus on Betsy and let's take one ghost at a time." I knew she meant the ghost of my past that I couldn't let go.

After a little chit-chat about other things in our lives and just visiting with each other, it was time for Jack Henry and I to leave.

"Can we just go home?" I asked after Jack had opened my car door. He was such a southern gentleman and I loved that. "I'm not hungry and I'm afraid I won't make good dinner company tonight."

"Of course," Jack Henry curled me into his arms, kissing the top of my head.

Chapter Five

"Oh no, you didn't get a call already this morning?"
Cheryl Lynne Doyle asked when she noticed I'd walked
into the coffeehouse. Her blond hair was neatly combed
into a low ponytail at the nape of her neck.

Cheryl was the owner of Higher Grounds Café. It was
the first and only coffeehouse in Sleepy Hollow. Cheryl
and I were classmates in high school and when she went off
to the big city to go to college she'd been sucked in by all
the fancy coffees and the environment that came with it.
Cheryl was used to getting everything in life that she
wanted. A coffee shop was no different. It was also a way
for her parents to get her out of a big city and back home in
Kentucky.

I had to admit that I was surprised at how well Cheryl
has taken to owning her own business. Though we weren't
friends in high school, we'd become friends as adults.

"Nope. No one has died that I know of." I assured her
because it was usually this early in the morning I'd show
up here to grab a big coffee after I'd gone to pick up a body
from a late night call.

That was the thing with being an undertaker. Many of
my funeral home clients had pre-need funeral
arrangements, which meant that they'd made their funeral
plans long before they died. For some reason, God only
knows, most people seemed to pass in the middle of the
night. I'd get the call and off I'd go. If I wasn't available,
Vernon picked up the emergency phone. Of course he got

all the police calls, but I generally knew about them first because of Jack Henry.

"Actually," I reached over the counter where she'd already poured my big cup of coffee. "I'm going to the library to do some research."

"Research?" She looked at me sideways. "On what?" she asked with a cautious tone.

"I hope it's on nursing homes." The familiar voice of Beulah Paige Bellefry chirped behind me.

My inner core shook. Hearing her this early was fingernails-on-a-chalkboard rough.

At five-foot-six, Beulah Paige was the epicenter of gossip since Ruthie had passed. It was like the baton was passed right on over to Beulah and she never had anything real nice to say about anyone.

"Excuse me?" I turned around and glared at her.

"Lookie yonder." She pointed her long thin finger to the outside.

"Now what?" I asked with a pit in my stomach when I saw Granny parking her moped in the bike rack in front of Higher Grounds and wearing a wedding dress.

"Like I said," Beulah's southern accent dripped with sarcasm, "I hope you're researching nursing homes because Zula Fae has lost her mind. Or getting married for the third time."

Before I could get past the line of customers and zig zag through the filled café tables inside Higher Grounds, Granny was inside the door with a bouquet of flowers over her head.

"Who's getting married next?" She twirled the flowers around and around her head and then flung them at me. "Congratulations Emma Lee and Jack Henry! You're next."

I caught the bouquet like a football. Leaves and petals fell off the stems where she'd hit me so hard with them.

"What is wrong with you? What do you have on?" I pulled her aside to one of the café tables in the corner and tried to not look at all the eyes on us.

"I remember that dress." Mable Claire's face beamed from one café table over.

"Looks like we need to talk about arrangements." Bea Allen Burns was enjoying this way too much.

"Over my dead body." Granny grabbed the flowers out of my hand and whacked Bea Allen with them.

"Stop it." I grabbed the flowers and profusely apologized to Bea Allen.

I really didn't mean the apology since Bea Allen Burns, owner of Burns Funeral Home, was my biggest competitor. She did everything in her power to monopolize all the deaths in Sleepy Hollow. It was really her brother and our current mayor, O'Dell Burns that we Raines had a problem with. Specifically over Granny's second husband, Earl Way Payne.

Ever since a mix up with Earl Way's funeral arrangement our families have been at odds. Mix up meaning Granny wasn't going to fulfill his wishes of being buried by Burns Funeral, so she went ahead and got him all dolled up and looking so handsome in the big picture window of Eternal Slumber. She figured O'Dell didn't have the guts to go in there and take the body. She figured wrong. Needless to say, O'Dell didn't waste no time pushing the church cart down the center aisle of Earl's funeral and packing him right on out of there. It had been a mess. Now Bea Allen and I continued the feud since she took over her brother's funeral home business after he was sworn in as mayor. Another sore subject with Granny.

"You look as pretty today in that as you did on your wedding day." Mable Claire grinned.

Bless Mable Claire's heart. She was so loyal to Granny. So loyal that she still wore the Vote For Zula For Mayor campaign pin on her shirt every day and the election had been over a year ago.

"Who's getting married?" Jack Henry stood under the dinging bell, signaling his arrival. He looked very amused with Granny.

"Apparently you are." Beulah broke the news. His amused look faltered.

"Oh Granny is playing silly." I smacked her in the chest with the flowers. "Now, go on back to the Inn and change out of that ridiculous dress."

"Wouldn't Emma Lee look so pretty in this silky cream wedding dress?" Granny did the step and stop, step and stop walk brides used to do when they walked down the aisle with the flowers firmly held up to her chest. "It might be a little outdated, but it's mine and it's something old." She turned and gave me a theatrical wink.

"Emma Lee would look good in a brown sugar sack." Jack Henry stepped aside as Granny continued her walk and stop routine out the door. "What was that all about?"

"Granny and her thirty-year-old joke I'm sure." It wasn't a secret around here that Granny said if you weren't married off by thirty, you were an old maid. I watched out the window as she zoomed off on her moped toward the Inn, regretting I'd even mentioned the ring I'd found in Jack Henry's coat pocket.

Technically, I didn't find it. It fell out and I quickly stuck it back in his pocket before he came back into my hospital room.

"She's a character." Jack Henry was doing a good job of throwing me off. I nodded.

"I'm going to grab a coffee and head on out to the office." He gave me a kiss. "What's your plan?"

"I wanted to grab a coffee and walk over to the library to see what I can find out about my little friend." I took a drink of the coffee and wished there was something a little stronger in it when I saw Granny do a loop around the square. She held onto the moped with one hand while she twirled the bouquet above her head before tossing it at the café door and gunning it. "Want to grab a drink later?"

"Drink?" Jack looked at me.

"I have a feeling a drink might be in order because it's gonna be a long day." I sucked in a deep breath.

"I'm outta here." Bea Allen patted Jack Henry on her way out. "Congratulations to the happy couple."

"We aren't. . ." I started to say but she walked out too fast. And I did notice Jack Henry just smiled.

Chapter Six

There was one thing I did know, no matter how much I tried to convince Granny to stop it with the wedding dress, I was going to lose. There was no sassing Granny when she had something in her head. Right now, me getting married was in her head.

There was a slight chill in the air. The horizon of fall was on the cusp of Sleepy Hollow and soon I'd be walking down the street with a Pumpkin Spiced Latte instead of a regular coffee. The library was a little piece away from the square past Sleepy Hollow Baptist, the only church in town.

Like the rest of the town, the library was small and in a clapboard house. It didn't lack books or access to anything new. The library had the latest in technology and Mayor Burns was very proud of that. In fact, it's how he got elected. Granny relied on loyalty against O'Dell where he relied on parents and their children's education. Part of his platform was growth in funding for the library and the local school. Granny's platform was. . .come to think of it, Granny hadn't even had a platform.

Of course my phone chirped from my bag that was strapped across my body as soon as I walked into the quiet library. Mazie Watkins's eyes flickered from behind the reference desk. It was her way of telling me to take it outside without even opening her mouth. When I retrieved it, I noticed it was Mary Anna, probably wanting to pick up her paycheck.

"Good morning, Mary Anna," I greeted her after I'd hit the green answer button and walked back out of the library.

"I'm so excited!" she screamed through the phone. "I've already got you down for a cut, color and brow wax."

"Brow wax?" I ran my finger over my eyebrows.

"Honey." Mary Anna scolded me. "The wedding of the century and our bride has to at least get those brows done. It might've looked good on Brooke Shields in the eighties, but that was then. You need a cut, color and wax. Maybe not just on the brows either. Where are you going on the honeymoon? We can discuss other waxing options later."

"Mary Anna, I think you've got this all wrong." Sheer panic hit me. If I didn't get Granny under control, she'd have a wedding tomorrow. "I'm not even engaged."

"But Zula called first thing this morning and made an appointment for the shower, rehearsal dinner and wedding." Her voice faded.

"Between me and you," I had to stop the train. "Granny might be losing her mind. Don't you think I'd have told everyone myself if I was getting married?"

"Poor Zula." Sadness held in her tone. "You know when she traded her perfectly good Toy-yota and got that moped, I wondered if she'd lost her mind. I'm so sorry. I'm sure Doc Clyde can give her something for it. After all, they're still dating, right?"

"Right they are." I smiled when I got the idea in my head. What if Granny and Doc Clyde got married. That'd keep her occupied. Whatever Zula Fae Raines Payne wanted, she got. "Zula Fae Raines Payne Clyde doesn't have a bad ring does it?"

"You are a stinker. But I have to say that I'm sad the rumors aren't true. You'd have made an excellent bride and mother." She clicked off the phone.

Mother? Did she say mother? I let out a long audible breath and tried to get myself into the right frame of mind to try to get to the bottom of Betsy's death.

"You do know that we ask you to turn off your cell phones when you enter the building." Mazie pushed a strand of her short brown wavy hair away from her mouth. Her olive skin and green eyes gave her a very exotic look.

She pointed to a sign that had an illustrated picture of a cell phone on it with a big red slash through it. "But then again, I never see you in here. In fact, I don't ever recall you coming in here."

"I've got some research to do." I flipped the little button on the side of my phone to silence it and stuck it back in my bag. "I'm going to use some of that funding Mayor got for us. The computers."

"You mean computer? As in one." She held up her finger and then my eyes followed it as she swept it across the room. "And we have a wait list to use it."

She slid a piece of paper across the reference desk and placed a pen on top of it. It looked like I was second on the list. I scribbled my name.

"What does that say?" she asked.

"My name." My voice hardened.

"You don't have very good penmanship," she noted before she hmm'd to herself and turned away.

The only other people in the library were the person on the computer and the person who must've been on the list before me. Out of the corner of my eye, Betsy appeared in the children's section. She took off running toward one of the beanbag chairs and fell in, then bringing her book above her head, she started to read.

I grabbed a book on my way over to act as though I was interested in reading something and opened it, pretending to read to myself, but really talking to Betsy.

"So you love to read." Not that it was a big revelation. She'd always carried around a book.

"I do. It helps me escape into far away places." Her little smile warmed the piece of my heart that knew she was precious, but my the other side of my heart ached knowing somewhere someone was missing her. "I guess you're going to get married on your birfday."

"No. No." I held the book up in front of my face and sat next to her on the beanbag. "I'm not getting married."

"But everyone's saying you're getting married. Are you going to forget about me? That's what she said. My mommy was going to forget about me. I think she forgot about me," her small voice faded and so did she.

"Betsy." I took the book down and looked around for her. "Who said your mommy was going to forget you?" I asked out loud. "Psst, Betsy," I called.

"Emma Lee, this is a quiet zone." Mazie didn't waste one second to reprimand me. "You're up." She snapped her fingers and pointed to the computer.

"Oh, sorry." I held the book up. "This is a great book."

"Beer crafting?" Mazie's brows lifted.

"Beer crafting?" I turned the cover around and noticed the book that I'd haphazardly picked up was just that. "Yeah. Jack Henry is interested." I lied and tucked my chin down so I didn't have to look at her on my way over to the computer.

There was a process to using the missing child database. Since I knew Betsy's first and middle names, I typed those in and immediately an article appeared from twenty years ago, almost to the date, with a photo of a much more vibrant Betsy Lynn Brady. A ten-year-old little girl from Lexington had gone missing from her mother's home. The article stated that her mother had woken up late. It was unusual because Betsy always crawled into bed with her and woke her up. When she woke up and Betsy wasn't in there, she immediately went to Betsy's room. Betsy was nowhere in the house. The housekeeper had been there but hadn't seen Betsy either. The housekeeper said that she thought Betsy had gone to her father's house or a sleepover.

"Are you printing?" Mazie called from the resource desk.

"Shhh." I reminded her and smiled so she knew I was joking.

"We are the only people in here. As a matter of fact, today has been the busiest we've been since school's been in." Mazie held up some papers. "Are you printing or not?"

"Yes." I watched as she read the headlines about the missing girl.

"I remember this case." She held up the papers. "Don't you remember our parents telling us to stay close to our homes in fear of getting abducted?"

"I don't." My parents didn't really have on the news or the TV. They claimed having dead bodies around our house was enough sadness and that they didn't expose us to any more than they had to, but when I read the article it didn't dawn on me that Betsy and I were the same age.

"They never found her." A sad sigh accompanied Mazie's turned down mouth. "My mother couldn't wait for the nightly news to come on to hear any updates."

"Was it national?" I asked.

"Yes. I remember my mother just crying and hugging me saying over and over how she couldn't imagine if it was me." Mazie stared off into space with no knowledge that the little girl she was talking about was right there staring back at her.

Chapter Seven

The Sleepy Hollow Police Station was on the outskirts of the square. It was the typical brick building with an flagpole in the middle of a circular drive with an American flag waving in the cool fall breeze.

"My mommy came to one of these places." Betsy stared out of the front seat of the hearse.

"In a hearse?" I asked. My heart dropped. I couldn't imagine doing a funeral for a little one. Luckily, I'd not had to do that.

"No. In a police station. They thought that my mommy hid me away but she didn't." Betsy's face greyed even more than her ghost form already was. "I tried to get her attention several times but she never looked at me. Maybe she was going to get rid of me when she got married."

"Why do you keep saying that?" I asked and parked the hearse on the side of the building in the visitor lot.

"She was going to get married. I don't think he wanted children." She tucked her chin to her chest and gripped the edges of her book before she faded away.

The one thing with my Betweener clients, they wanted help but only when it was convenient for them. If the conversation got heavy, they'd just ghost away and I hated that part of the gig.

"I'm dying to know why you are here." One of the officers said when he saw me and laughed. "Get it. Dying."

I pretended to laugh, but inwardly cringed. Funeral home humor was never funny to me.

"Is Jack Henry here?" I asked.

The officer pointed behind him. "Should be in his office."

"Thanks." I took it as a go ahead to walk back there.

Jack was sitting behind the desk and reading some papers. He waved me in when I knocked on the door.

"Wow." He got up and walked over to hug me. "You never come here. What do I owe the pleasure?"

"Betsy Lynn Brady is a cold case from Lexington." I opened my bag and took out the articles I'd printed off at the library. "She went missing almost twenty years ago to the day. Her mother was a suspect along with the maid. Neither of those leads panned out. The mom's fiancé was questioned but was never a suspect. Betsy keeps telling me that someone said to her that when her mom got married, she was going to get rid of Betsy."

"Abduction?" Jack Henry looked over the papers. "Maybe the kidnapper told Betsy that to go with him."

"Maybe?" My head tilted to the side. "Mazie Watkins said that she remembers this being a national case when she was a little girl. Do you?"

He took a minute to read over it.

"I vaguely remember something about it, but not much. I was so busy with sports that we were rarely home for the news, but I do recall some of the moms at the ballpark talking about it." He laid the papers on his desk.

"Well." My brows lifted.

"Well what?" he asked.

"Reopen the case." I jabbed at the paperwork. "Obviously, Betsy was killed or she wouldn't be here with me."

Betsy stood next to Jack Henry, her hands at her sides. A book in one hand. Her body twisted back and forth.

"I'd marry him." She blushed. "And he's going to help me."

"Emma Lee, I don't do cold cases." Jack Henry Ross's words weren't pleasing to me. "And it's not our district."

"Then who does do cold cases around here?" I asked and got up from the chair. "Let's go Betsy."

"She's here?" Jack looked around.

"Yeah. She thinks you're going to help her." I looked at her. "He's not," I said flatly.

"Emma Lee, that's a whole 'nother unit up in Lexington." Jack Henry peeked around my shoulder to make sure no one was looking at us before he leaned in and whispered, "The girl is this little girl in the photo?"

"Yes." There was no denying it. "A little more ghost-like and pale, but yes."

"Let me look into it and see what I can come up with." He lifted his hand to my face. "I would hate to disappoint you but I've got to have something to go on."

"Like what?" I asked.

"Like where is her body? Bones by now," he restated. "But where is the location? I'll get out there and look around."

"Something about a barn." I shrugged. "Do you remember anything about you and Mr. Whiskers?" I asked.

"No. He kept me company when I was alone. I was scared. Especially when the flames came." She looked up at me. Her eyes popped. "There was smoke and flames. I couldn't breathe." She lifted her hand and put it across her nose. "Mr. Whiskers laid on my face to filter the smoke."

"She said there was smoke and flames. Google barn fires around that time." It seemed like a reasonable suggestion.

Jack hurried back behind his desk and as he typed away, I secretly prayed that as much as a barn fire and dying that way would be painful, not knowing where your

child had gone had to be even more painful for her mother.
Unless her mother had any hope that Betsy was still alive.

"Right here." He pointed to the screen of his computer.
I walked behind him and looked at it over his shoulder.
"And it's in Sleepy Hollow County too."

"What does that mean?" I asked.

"You know the old strip mall out halfway to
Lexington?" He referred to an old farm that'd been turned
into an Adidas outlet, Dress Barn outlet along with a few
other stores that seemed to be popping up in the south
along with a few restaurants. "It went out of business when
we were like sixteen or something. Now it's abandoned."

"Yes." I shook my head.

"There was an old barn out there. The owner who sold
the land to the developer had set fire to the barn instead of
having it bulldozed. I remember something about this
because it had to do with a fire. The county got him for
arson since he didn't have the right permit to do it and he
should've had the fire department there and everything.
The moms at the ball field talked about that too."

"You don't think it could be the same fire do you?" I
asked.

"Only one way to find out." He grabbed his keys,
badge, and gun holster. "Want to ride in a cop's car?" he
teased. "I'll let you turn on the siren."

"You are so sexy." I giggled and grabbed his hand.

"Ewww." Betsy moved her hand from her nose to over
her eyes.

Unfortunately, Jack Henry wouldn't let me turn on the
siren as he'd promised, but he did let me cuddle up next to
him on the way over to the abandoned strip mall. Quite a
distance behind the mall were still the remains of what
looked to be a charred barn.

"That's it." Betsy shivered and took off running toward the barn. "Mr. Whiskers lived here first."

Abruptly I stopped and watched as Betsy ran. The grass was tall and she was barely visible. When I squinted, I could make out Mr. Whiskers's tail bopping along the top of the grass as if he were trying to keep up with her.

"What's wrong?" Jack asked and looked off toward the barn.

"Betsy and Mr. Whiskers said this is it. Apparently Mr. Whiskers was just a barn cat that she met here." The thought of the owner not knowing a little girl was hiding inside made me sad. "The owner." I gulped and followed Jack through the weeds and grass with each high-step. "Do you think it's murder if he didn't know she was in there?"

I asked this because I knew that once the killer was brought to justice, then Betsy would cross over to the other side and Mr. Whiskers to what the living called the Rainbow Bridge for animals. Right now, she wasn't going anywhere but in the barn.

"So she's not gone?" His brows furrowed. "Maybe her parents need closure."

"Yeah. Maybe." I gnawed at the thought of having to tell her parents. "I just can't imagine telling them after all these years. What if they are still holding out hope that she's alive like all those other cases over the past few years?"

"The reality is that we can't think that way. We have to or at least I have to think that we are giving them closure. It's the only way I can do my job." He pulled the flashlight off of his utility belt and shined it all over the remaining charred wood.

We were losing daylight fast and I just couldn't leave unless we found her or at least part of her remains.

"We played over here a lot and," Betsy stopped, looked down at Mr. Whiskers as he pawed something. She simply pointed to a board that looked like a beam from the barn ceiling.

"Under there. Betsy is pointing under there," I told Jack Henry.

As he positioned himself on the uneven boards, I could barely bring myself to look.

"It's okay." Betsy's sweet voice assured me. "See." She put her hands out. "I'm fine." Mr. Whiskers danced around her feet.

"I guess we better get forensics out here." Jack Henry shined his light down on the ground where he'd moved the beam. "It looks like we have some skeletal remains."

There were no words to say about what I knew he was going to find. The only thing I felt was sick and empty, just like the day I found Charlotte Rae.

Chapter Eight

An old wood-paneled beat-up station wagon pulled up to the scene. Behind the wheel was Fluggie Callahan, the editor-in-chief, owner and only employee of *Sleepy Hollow Gazette*. Her sandy blond hair was pulled up in a scrunchie. The stray hairs were tucked tight around her head with bobby pins. Her white lashes were magnified under her big-rimmed glasses.

"News sure does travel fast." Jack Henry's eyes were covered with the Rayban mirrored sunglasses.

"News and gossip." I could hear it. The whiz of the moped. It was distinct like a train whistle that could be heard from miles away. Only the conductor was Granny.

The forensic team looked like an archeological dig team. They'd roped off the area and used what looked to be paint brushes as they slowly and meticulously brushed along the area where the small skull was sticking up from the ground. Betsy and Mr. Whiskers continued to stand off a little bit in the distance.

Fluggie, on the other hand, had gotten out of her car and clipped on her fanny pack. She wore a long-sleeved white tee that was tucked in her pants that were about three inches too short and pulled plum up to her armpits. She had on a pair of white tennis shoes and a camera hung around her neck.

Granny wasted no time driving right up between Jack Henry and me. I was never so happy to see her in regular clothes.

"Bless their heart. Who was it?" Granny pulled off her aviator goggles and black helmet. Her red hair sprang out. Her eyes twinkled with curiosity.

"We got a tip that it could possibly be Betsy Lynn Brady," I said, but didn't take my eyes off the scene after I caught some movement other than dusting away the dirt.

"We've got a book." One of the officers held up a children's book by the corner.

Another officer rushed over with an evidence bag and held it open.

"Be careful with my book." Betsy stomped. "I love my books! Emma!"

Our eyes met. There was a sadness that I'd not recognized in her eyes over the past few months. Maybe it was too much for a little girl to see what'd happened to her. It was then that I followed her eyes to a police car that was pulling up with the lights on but not the siren.

"Who?" Granny nudged me. "We don't know no Betsy."

"Do you remember a little girl that went missing from Lexington when I was about ten?" I asked and kept on eye on the police car and wondered who had needed an escort to the site.

Out of the corner of my eye, Fluggie was taking all sorts of photos of the landscape. She also walked toward the police car.

"Excuse me." Jack Henry put his hand out and stalked toward Fluggie.

"Who's in the car?" Granny rubbernecked. "Betsy who?"

The air had turned a bit chilly. The sun was starting to set and sent a light yellow glow behind the trees that lined the property.

"When I was ten, there was a little girl who'd gone missing." I watched as Jack Henry said something to Fluggie. She nodded her head and rested the camera on her chest. She opened her fanny pack and pulled out a notepad and pen.

"I do remember something about that and I think her mama was the suspect." Just as the words left Granny's mouth, a woman stepped out of the police cruiser.

Her eyes were red around the ridges. She held a Kleenex up to her face. Betsy ghosted to her and then over to me.

"Is that my mommy?" Betsy's voice cracked as if she were about to cry. "Tell me, Emma," she begged.

I sucked in a deep breath and tried not to pay attention to her because Granny was standing there.

"That looks like my mommy but she's so old." The little girl looked up at me. "Please talk to me," she begged and sniffed in and out of her nose.

With my lips curled in, I looked down at her and did a long blink. When I reopened them, Betsy wasn't there.

"I think her mom was a suspect, but nothing came of it. I couldn't imagine she did that to her only child." I watched as Jack Henry stood with her. I could only imagine what he was saying to her. She nodded her head and blotted her eyes as he talked.

"Where did the lead come from?" Granny was curious now. "And do you think it was the killer finally getting a conscience after all these years? If this happened to one of mine, I'd wallop on whoever did it. They'd not need a trial. I'd hold my own court. Me and my forty-five." Granny's brow rose.

"I'm not sure how Jack Henry found out," I lied and looked around to see if I could see where Betsy had gone.

She was pretty upset with the fact that twenty years had passed. In her world, she was still ten years old and her life was the same. The police officer brought the book over to the Betsy's mom and she collapsed into Jack Henry's strong arms.

Fluggie wasted no time throwing her notepad on the ground, sticking the pen behind her ear, and grabbing the camera to get some action photos. My heart dropped and my insides cringed. Another officer saw Fluggie and stalked toward her with his hands up. He spouted something to her and she shouted back something about her rights.

"Hurry it up boys, we're burnin' daylight." Jack Henry peeled the glasses off his face and looked over the crime scene.

"Lord have mercy," Granny *tsked* as the police car with Betsy's mom passed us on the way out of the scene.

Jack Henry was going to stay at the scene a little longer than he'd anticipated. He suggested an officer take me back to the funeral home, but Granny chirped in that she had another soft helmet in the storage compartment underneath her moped seat. Jack was more than entertained and happy to coax Granny on and for me to ride with her back to Sleepy Hollow.

"I'll get you back," I warned him when he bent down to kiss me goodbye.

"I hope so." He winked with a sexy smile that made any part of me trying to get mad at him falter.

"Hold on!" Granny yelled above the moped motor and gunned it by gripping the throttle and twisting it all the way toward her.

I jerked back and grabbed her behind the waist, praying I wouldn't fall off. I had to be nuts riding with her. I'd never done it and I wasn't even sure if she had insurance on the thing. She didn't care. Zula Fae Raines Payne did exactly what she wanted to do.

Instead of her taking me to Eternal Slumber, she pulled the moped up in the middle of the Inn next to the large oak tree.

"I figured since you don't have no funeral clients, you can have some supper with me and Hettie before we do a little night yoga." Her brows wiggled.

She bent down and grabbed the large chain that she used to put around the tree and her moped. She clipped the big lock in place, took a step back, brushed her hands together and looked at her handiwork.

"I have no idea why you don't just put your moped in the shed instead of chaining it up." I gestured toward the small shed at the end of the small gravel parking lot next to the Sleepy Hollow Inn.

"Are you kidding me?" She snarled and peeled the goggles off of her face. "The yahoos that like to climb them caves and caverns sometimes have too much to drink or smoke that weed."

It sounded so funny when Granny talked about recreational drugs.

"They'd be more than happy to steal anything and everything." She nodded. "My moped being one of them."

"Did I miss something? Because we don't have a high crime rate or tourists." The only time I knew of crime was when I had Betweener clients.

"You never know. Always got to be prepared." She huffed and scurried onto the porch where a few guests were enjoying Granny's cocktail hour she offered to inn guests before supper.

Hettie Bell was in the dining room setting the linens when we walked in. Granny had her particular way to set a table.

"Go on in there and help Hettie. That whole bones being found thing made me late on making my pork chops."

She gave me a slight push toward the dining room French doors and she shut them behind me. The doors were left closed until it was time to open them up for the dining crowd. Granny had a little chalkboard that hung off the door knob with the times the dining room was open. The chalkboard clinked against the closed doors.

"I'll never get tired of this view." I still marveled at the mountainous caves that were the backdrop for the Inn.

This was what made the Sleepy Hollow Inn so valuable. It had the prettiest view of all.

"It's the perfect spot to relax after a long day of hiking." Hettie walked over and stood next to me to enjoy the view. "I'm so glad I don't have to clean that wall of windows."

The dining room's back wall was just one big window.

"Your reception is going to be so pretty here." Hettie tucked a piece of her growing-out bangs behind her ear and a fistful of silverware in the other hand. "I'm so excited you agreed to do prenatal yoga."

"Whoa." There were two things that made alarm bells go off in my head. "Reception? Prenatal yoga?"

"Namaste." She did a lovely bow but not lovely enough to convince me to do any sort of yoga. Hettie wasn't a local. She moved to Sleepy Hollow a couple of years ago and completely changed her look. Once she was a Goth-type but now she's all into her body, mind, spirit and my business thanks to Granny.

"Granny," I sighed and rolled my eyes so hard it hurt. "First off, I'm not engaged." I lifted my hand in the air to show her no ring. "Secondly, I'm nowhere near having a baby."

Goodness gracious no. I took the silverware from her hand and busied myself by walking around the tables to make sure each table had the appropriate number of place settings. Hettie kept her mouth shut and walked around to straighten the linen napkins.

"Are these new?" I noticed Granny had switched out the maroon linen napkins to a white. "Granny hates using white napkins."

"Mmmhmmm." Hettie offered a thin smile.

"And did she take out some tables?" I asked, trying to get Hettie to talk to me. "Listen," I turned back to her. "I'm sorry that I took my frustration with Granny out on you. I know you're only doing what she asked you to do. Doesn't she realize you have Pose and Relax to run?"

"I don't mind helping out Zula Fae. She did give me my first job and I have to say that it's fun to come here and rub elbows with tourists." She stopped in front of the windows. Her head tilted to the side and she signed, loudly. "Even after a couple of years, I'm still new to the caves and caverns. I learn something new in here from a customer every week. Besides," she came back to the present and shrugged, "my classes are early morning and a couple at night. But not tonight."

"What's going on tonight?" I asked, knowing that I've been out of the loop all day.

Without even answering me, she looked at the french doors. Granny stood there with a big white cake and lit sparklers in her hands with Beulah Paige, Mary Anna Hardy, Mable Claire, Marla Marie Teater, Fluggie Callahan, and Cheryl Lynne Doyle behind her. All of them holding presents.

"Happy engagement shower!" They sing-songed in unison and walked in.

"What the hell?" I fumed under my breath.

"I understand you aren't engaged, but please just don't make a scene. Zula Fae will have Doc Clyde over here in a minute," Hettie warned.

Chapter Nine

"Doesn't Granny look happy?" I asked Doc Clyde when he showed up for supper. Granny was in the middle of the gifts, looking like it was her shower.

He'd no clue Granny had closed the dining room, though she did have a barbeque set up outside for her guests in the side yard. She'd gone to great lengths while I was in the dining room helping Hettie Bell set up for what was an engagement party for me, the unengaged Emma Lee Raines.

While I was inside, Granny had The Southern Soiree put up a couple white tents with two buffet tables of the best barbeque. They also had southern slaw, flat green beans, biscuits along with cornbread. They'd also brought the two-layer white engagement cake that had simple white daisy flowers on the top.

"She loves a good wedding." It wasn't a bad idea to put the thought in Doc Clyde's mind. Maybe I could turn this whole wedding mix-up into a wedding for her. The idea was brilliant really. "She's so young and spry. I hope you. . .er. . ." I pretended to have a Freidan slip. "I mean, I hope Granny gets to experience another wedding in her life. She's had such trauma the last few months," my voice took a dip with sadness, "that it'd really help get her mind off our sorrow."

"You think Zula wants to get married again?" Doc Clyde fidgeted.

"Absolutely." Maybe absolutely was a teeny-tiny bit of an exaggeration. "She's seventy-nine years old. Still spry and feisty as ever."

Both of us turned our attention toward her. She was stuck in the middle of the gossiping women. Her bright red lipstick matched her bright red short hair. When she noticed us staring, she gave a wink and a wave, followed up by blowing a kiss to Doc Clyde, to which he turned as red as her fake L'Oreal hair dye that she claimed Mary Anna insisted on putting on. Knowing Granny, it was the other way around.

"I'm worried about the hives that she's got." Doc reminded me about Granny's reaction to the ghost cat.

"Hmmm." I pinched my lips together.

"You said you ain't getting married to Jack Henry." Beulah Paige had made her way over and rudely interrupted Doc and me.

Not surprised.

Her fake lashes drew a shadow down her fake tanned face when her eyes dipped to get a look at my hand.

"Nope." I raised it so she didn't have to work so hard to see if there was a ring. Though I'd have been thoroughly entertained if a lash fell off.

"Don't tell me this is one of them marrying myself things because I saw that on the TV and it was weird." She fiddled with the strand of pearls around her neck. "Girl married herself." She *tsked*. "Ridiculous if you ask me. They just want a present." She lifted her finger off her pearls and pointed to the gifts. "Which reminds me that if this isn't a real shower, then I'm taking my gift back."

"By all means." I laughed. Though my birthday was this week. Even though I wasn't engaged, it was kind of fun to feel like it for a minute.

"Okay! Time to open presents." Granny clapped her hands.

Beulah and I walked over to the group. When she reached over to take her gift off the table, Granny smacked her hand away.

"You Indian giver." Granny glared.

"If I wasn't part Native American, Zula, I'd be offended." Beulah rubbed her hand.

"Get over it. Besides, what part is Naaa-tive American? You're a regular at Tan Your Hide." Granny's words had bite.

"If it weren't for Emma Lee, I'd leave." Beulah stood there and lied right in front of all of our faces.

"Does that mean you're switching your preneed funeral arrangements?" I asked knowing she was a Burns person, meaning she had all her arrangements with Bea Allen Burns.

"Did y'all hear about them bones found over at the rundown mall?" Cheryl Lynne Doyle changed the subject before my fake shower became a brawl.

It wasn't long ago that Granny and Beulah had a knockdown, drag-out throw down in Higher Grounds. According to Cheryl Lynne, it wasn't good for business.

"Mm-hmm." Granny nodded with confidence. "It's that girl missing from twenty years ago. 'Member that?" she asked as if she knew all about it.

"How do you know?" Mable Claire asked as she waddled and jingled over to the group. Mable was short and had fuller hips. Her pockets were always filled with coins. Mable had never had children of her own and she loved to give a penny here and there to the children she'd pass on the street.

Granny handed me a present.

"Ask Emma Lee. She knows all about it from Jack Henry." Granny knew just enough to start the gossip mill to get it to circulate around Sleepy Hollow.

Everyone looked at me. I held the small box in my lap.

"Some sort of tip." I shrugged and popped the bow off the present.

"One child!" Granny trilled with delight and grabbed the broken bow out of my hand.

"What?" My jaw dropped at how excited she'd gotten over a bow.

"It's an old wives' tale." Leave it up to Hettie Bell to know the rules of fake engagement showers. "Every bow you breaks represents how many babies you and Jack Henry will have."

"I'm not getting married." Exhaustion laced my words. "I'm not having babies."

"You're gonna be thirty years old." Granny patted her pockets. "Where's my glue?"

"Glue? What are we doing with glue?" I asked.

It was as if Hettie had been in on this whole engagement thing from the beginning. She handed Granny a paper plate and a bottle of glue. Granny glued the bow on the plate.

"Now, what's in the box?" Granny brought the attention back to me.

Everyone ooh'd and aww'd over the cat pajamas that were the least sexy thing to get a soon-to-be-bride, not that I was going to be one, but in a real shower I'm not sure I'd want these particular pj's.

"Thank you, Fluggie." I held them up for everyone to see.

"I heard you got you a cat." She shoved a piece of the cake in her mouth.

"You got a cat?" As if the words made Granny itch, she reached down to her ankles and scratched them. "No wonder I've got the itches. I'm allergic to cats."

"I didn't get a cat," I said to clear the air.

"Someone said that they saw you down at the Buy and Fly buying up different cans of cat food." Fluggie had her sleuthing hat on. "Just like there were cat bones at the barn."

Fluggie stared at me a little too long. She had a way of trying to figure out how I knew things. Her eyes narrowed. Her chin slightly tilted to the side like she had a thought that was dying to come out.

"Nope. No cat. And I don't know anything about a barn cat." I grabbed another present.

"I didn't say barn cat. I said cat found with the bones of Betsy Lynn Brady," she said. "Wasn't it you that had Jack Henry go out there? I mean, why would he want to go out there?"

"I told you. A lead." I popped another bow and just threw it Granny's way as she bounced with excitement. Her fingers did the "gimmie" gesture.

"I went down to the station to go through the calls and there doesn't seem to be any sort of record of a lead." She took another bite of her cake. "I find it interesting that this would be the seventh case Jack Henry has taken you on."

"Taken me on?" I asked and opened the box to take out a see through cream nighty with feather trim.

Immediately I knew whom it was from. Marla Marie Teater. She was, after all, the former beauty queen and owned a sort of grooming school for girls who wanted to enter and win pageants. There was also a tube of hemorrhoid cream in the box. She claimed that if you applied it to the wrinkles and lines on your face, it'd tighten it right on up like it did a hemorrhoid.

"Va-va-voom!" Jack Henry smiled from the french doors of the dining room. He obviously liked what he saw. "Is this a surprise birthday party?"

"No, silly!" Granny jumped up quicker than a jackrabbit. "It's your engagement party."

"My what?" Jack Henry's eyes practically popped out of his head and his jaw dropped.

I hung my head.

Chapter Ten

"I called you a few times last night." Jack Henry had picked me up to go see Betsy's mom and ask her a few questions. He figured Betsy might show up and be able to offer some unanswered questions.

After the made up shower Granny had given me, Jack Henry was somewhat floored and shocked with the idea of an engagement party and being engaged to someone who he'd not asked to marry. Of course there wasn't any explanation other than Granny had flat out lost all her marbles and playing along had been the best thing to do since she'd already had it catered.

"I was tired," I lied and yawned from the other side of his police cruiser. "But hopefully this will pep me up."

Seeing Jack Henry first thing in the morning was a delight. Seeing Jack Henry first thing in the morning with a big cup of coffee was a treat. A much needed treat.

"Cheryl Lynne was somewhat amused this morning when I picked up the coffees." He was being kind because we both knew that we were the topic of gossip around here. Us and the bones of Betsy Lynn and Mr. Whiskers. "What on earth gave Zula Fae the idea we were engaged?"

The idea of coming clean to Jack Henry about me knowing about the ring wasn't a pleasant thought. It's not how a woman thinks the big proposal was going to happen and it certainly wasn't how I'd imagined it.

Jack Henry gripped the wheel of the cruiser as we drove under the canopy of fall colors on the road to Lexington.

"Me." I closed my eyes and laid my head back on the headrest of the passenger seat. "When I was in the hospital six months ago after Charlotte died, I'd moved your jacket. A velvet ring box fell out and of course Charlotte and I thought it was for me. The thought of getting married without her isn't something I can do just yet. I sort of told Granny that I thought you were going to propose. It wasn't enough for her to listen to me, she had to go one step further."

"Velvet ring box?" Jack Henry acted as if he didn't know what I was talking about.

"Yes. I'm sorry. I should've told you that I knew. And I've been waiting for you to get down on one knee for the last six months." It did feel good getting it off my shoulders.

He veered off the road and pulled over onto the shoulder. He shifted the gear into park and turned his body toward me.

"Emma Lee." He put his hand out and set it on mine. I gulped knowing this was the big moment. Now that he knew I knew, there was no reason for him not to ask.

"It's just too soon," I blurted out. "I do love you. I do. But. . ."

"Shhhh." He put his finger up to my lips. "That ring box wasn't for you."

"Huh?" My nose curled.

"It was my mom's. She'd sent it into the jewelers to have a diamond reset and I just picked it up for her while I was in town." He stared at my expression. He took his hand off of mine and ran it through his hair. "I love you. I do and I know you'll make a wonderful wife. But I also know you well enough to know that you aren't ready to get married or be married to a cop."

"How can you say that?" I asked. My heart was aching. How had I misread the clues. I was such an idiot and I felt so stupid.

"Look at you," he noted. "You've been torn up over a ring box for six months. You weren't even going to say yes if I did ask."

"I might've." There was a big lump in my throat that I was trying to choke down.

"You weren't. You just said it was too soon. Besides." He looked down in his lap. There was a long silence that was uncomfortable. "Remember that job a year ago that'd come up with the state police?"

"Yeah." I rolled my eyes.

His mother had really pushed for him to take the job and when he didn't, she blamed it all on me, making my relationship with her a little strained.

"I've been recommended again. I've felt your distance for the past six months and I've seriously thought about taking it." He could've pulled out his gun and shot me and I wouldn't have been as shocked as I was in this moment.

"Emma," he said my name in the way that made my toes curl and heart flutter. "Emma. Please. Emma, look at me."

"Did Granny's antics have anything to do with making this decision?" I swallowed and put the coffee cup in the holder.

Suddenly coffee didn't seem to sit well in my stomach. There was a fine line between Granny and Jack Henry.

"Absolutely not. I'd ask you to marry me right now if I knew your head was into it." His words were as soft as his kiss and I wanted neither of them. "When I do ask you to marry me, and I will, I want all of you. Not just part of you."

I nodded to get this conversation over with. Of course I didn't understand my feelings. He was right on the one hand that I wasn't in any mental place to plan a wedding, but my heart was all in when it came to knowing I wanted to be his wife. It's all I've ever dreamed of since the first day I saw him at school so many years ago.

"And I've not made any decision on the job." He turned back in his seat and pulled the gearshift into drive. "No one knows but you."

I settled back into the seat for a long day ahead.

"You okay?" Jack Henry rubbed my back as we waited at the front door of Betsy's mom's home.

I twisted away and looked back at the cruiser parked along the curb of the modest neighborhood. His hand dropped.

"I'm good, thank you kindly." I used my good southern manners Granny said would serve me well. I wasn't good. I was about a minute from a total breakdown.

At least in the back of my broken heart, there had been a brief spark of a silver lining that Jack Henry was just waiting for the perfect moment to propose. Now there wasn't any hope at a ring or even the continuation of a relationship. If he thought I was going to just wait around while he played cop all over the bluegrass state, he had another thing coming to him. Yep. The more I thought about it the angrier I got.

"Can I help you?" Betsy's mom stood behind the screened storm door. The wrinkles around her eyes softened when she realized it was Jack Henry. "I'm sorry." She apologized and opened the door.

The soothing sound of the creaking hinges played in my ears. Many times, Charlotte and I would bolt through the funeral home back door when it was time for supper and the screen door would creak before it smacked after we ran in.

"Emma Lee?" Jack called after me. He'd already stepped inside and I hadn't even noticed. "Betsy?" he whispered.

"No." I shook my head. "Another ghost."

His eyes popped and I simply smiled. Before a few minutes ago, I'd have told Jack Henry my exact thoughts and what I was thinking, but now something had changed in me.

"Let's do the job." I planted a sweet smile on my face but my insides were burning up. I was here to do my Betweener job and that meant getting Betsy to the other side. I was going to do my job and do it well. Another thing Granny told me, Emma Lee, you've got to look like a girl, act like a lady, think like a man, and work like a dog.

Chapter Eleven

"I'm sorry, where are my manners." Kay Brady had invited us in to sit on her couch in the family room. "Would you like a coffee or a tea?"

"No, ma'am." Jack Henry shook his head.

"I'd love a coffee. The one on the way here wasn't very good." I smiled and wiggled my shoulders.

"I've got a fresh pot." She stood up from the chair across from the couch. "I'll be right back."

"Little cream to color," I called after her, crossed my legs, and wrapped my hand around my knee.

"You shouldn't have coffee since I'm not sure she isn't a suspect. We are here for an interview." Instructions from Jack Henry weren't sitting well with me.

"You are here for an interview. I'm here to help Betsy cross over." I reminded him of our two very distinct jobs. "Isn't that right, Betsy?"

The little girl had been sitting on the arm of her mother's chair. Betsy smiled and nodded. Mr. Whiskers was curled up on the small rug in front of the front door. I eased back on the couch and ran my hand across the old fabric that looked like it'd been a fabric that matched curtains in the sixties.

"What's with the attitude?" Jack Henry pulled back and looked at me. His brows furrowed.

"No attitude. Just doing my job." I laughed. "What do you want me to do? Hug and kiss on you? We." I gestured between us. "Might not be a we."

Before he could say anything, Kay had walked back into the room with two cups of coffee.

"Are you sure you don't want one?" She asked Jack.

"No thank you. But thank you for taking the time to see me and Emma this morning." There he went with the southern charm and smile that reeled me in so long ago and was breaking my heart now.

Concentrate. Concentrate. I had to remind myself.

"Can you tell me exactly what happened the day of Betsy's disappearance?" I asked.

"Yes." It was like a cloud crossed over her face as she stared off into space. "That morning everything was great. Sharon was cleaning the house and getting it ready for the wedding that weekend. Kevin had been working so much so that he'd be able to take off for the two week honeymoon." She smiled as if she remembered something happy. "We were going to get married, take Betsy with us on the honeymoon for the first week. Betsy was going to fly home the second week so Kevin and I could have our own honeymoon. My mother was going to keep her."

"Did you live here?" I looked around at the family room.

There didn't seem to be anything new here. All of the furniture looked like it'd seen better days. Much better days. But who was I to judge? I lived in a freakin' funeral home.

"No. We lived in Kevin's mansion." She smiled. "He owned Rent a Room and made millions."

"Oh. Yeah." I nodded. "I remember those stores. The commercials."

I even remembered Kevin Allen. He was on the commercials spouting off how it was easy to rent his furniture with no down payment. He would wear silly hats and glasses to get your attention. It worked. Kevin Allen was a household name.

"You couldn't be any older than Betsy would be now." Kay's eyes circled around my face.

"No. Betsy and I were the same age." I knew she and I were thinking the same thing. That she could be my mother.

"It's hard to imagine my little pumpkin being a grown-up woman like yourself." Her head tilted. Her face softened. She pushed back a piece of hair off of her neck. The same piece of hair Betsy was playing with by putting it back on her mother's neck to tickle her. "I swear. This piece of hair has given me fits since Betsy died. She used to play with my hair and tickle me. I swear she's here sometimes."

Jack Henry scooted up on the seat uneasily and looked at me.

"Died? Since she died?" he asked. "It wasn't until yesterday that we truly knew it was her bones. How did you know she was not still alive somewhere?"

"I'm sorry officer." She glared at Jack. "I looked for my daughter for years. At some point it's just easier to think that she's dead and not coming back. It's easier to think that she's in heaven with my mother than living under a stranger's roof. Someone who took her." Her words had a harsh tone. "If you are insinuating that I killed my daughter like they did twenty years ago, then you can leave. I will take another polygraph test and will cooperate in any way to find who did this to my daughter. But as for your snide remarks, they aren't welcome in this house."

"I'm sure Sheriff Ross didn't mean anything, did you?" I looked at him.

"No, ma'am. I'm sorry for your loss. We just want to bring this cold case to a closure for you and your family. Is your husband around?" he asked.

"I never got married." She looked down at her hands and picked at the bed of her nails. "Truthfully, Kevin never wanted children. I worked for him in the office and we had a whirlwind romance. Betsy was ten and she was a good girl. Kevin didn't take on the father role, but that was okay. They got along well and he treated her good."

"He was mean." Betsy scowled. "I'm so glad Mommy didn't marry him."

"Did Betsy like him?" I asked.

"She did." Then Kay's brows knotted. "I guess she did. She never said anything."

"I did too. I told you he was mean and you blew me off. Then he didn't let me order dessert when we would go out to eat." Betsy spouted off things that were trivial, but I kept them in the back of my head.

"Why didn't you get married?" It seemed to me that if he wasn't fond of children, with Betsy missing he'd be happier.

"Me." She tucked her chin to her chest. "After Betsy," *ahem*, she cleared her throat, "I couldn't focus. I couldn't sleep. I started to drink and take pills. My world had completely turned upside down. My mom put me in a facility about a year after Betsy. . ." Her eyes teared. "I can't even bring myself to this day to say missing, disappeared, kidnapped, or killed."

"I understand." I reached out with the hand that didn't have the mug in it and patted her leg.

Charlotte wasn't my daughter, but she was my only sister. I understood a little bit of what she was saying and I certainly could feel the pain. After all these years, it looked as if she were feeling the loss all over again.

"Did the police interview Kevin as a suspect?" Jack Henry interjected.

Kay shot him a look. It was his insensitivity that she clearly didn't like.

"I think what Sheriff Ross is trying to say is that policing has come a long way. With the new DNA testing and some new forensic equipment, the cold case is reopened as a homicide. We'd like to know everything from that time in your life. Including Kevin's involvement." I offered a sincere smile.

"I'll be right back." She stood up and left the room.

"Policing?" Jack Henry asked. "You mean investigating?"

"Whatever." I rolled my eyes. "Could you be any more insensitive to her pain? She clearly is still upset and you could ease up a bit."

"Here." Kay walked back into the room. "Here is his cell phone information. He and I still keep in touch, though after some time we'd decided to go our separate ways." Kay looked off.

"Thank you." She offered the paper to me. I took it and handed it over to Jack. "Can you recall if Betsy was upset? Was there a reason for her to run to the barn?"

"No. She was so excited about putting on her princess dress for the wedding. Though." Kay's eyes teared. "A few days before, she did ask if Kevin wanted her to be his daughter and she continued to ask if things were going to change."

"Were they?" I asked.

"I told her that we were going to continue to live in the house and it would be ours. She could have sleepovers, swim in the pool, maybe even get a horse for the barn that Kevin never used." That put a smile on her face. "He had that big ole house and no love to fill it. He used to joke that it was so quiet before we came."

"He yelled at me when I was loud." Betsy eyes darkened. "He told Mommy I was too loud and it needed to be quiet when he got home from work so he could rest. He smelled stinky."

"Was there a time that Kevin wanted it to be quiet?" I tried to phrase it as if I'd just come up with the question and Betsy hadn't told me what happened.

"Oh no. He loved the noise." She took a deep breath and exhaled. "Of course he'd come home tired sometimes from a long day. But we were all tired."

"He wanted to send me off to school. Don't you remember?" Betsy asked her mom as though she could hear her. "Mommy? Mommy!" Frustrated, she disappeared.

"You didn't hear anything the morning she disappeared?" I wanted to make sure.

"Usually I'm a very light sleeper but I was exhausted from the night before." Kay's eyes softened. "Betsy had been asking a lot of questions about the house and if Kevin loved her. She continued to question her place in the new life we were going to have. Kevin had talked me into a little girl's party here. We had a bouncy house and the pool was still open since there was a heater. Betsy didn't care if it was warm or cold. She shivered the whole time. There was a petting zoo too." There was a weak smile on her face. "Betsy was so happy. She thanked me so much. And then she was gone."

She looked off into the distance. Her stillness was silent. There was so much sadness.

"Well, I'm sure you've got things to do today." I stood up and looked at Jack Henry.

He looked a bit confused.

"We'll be in touch." I put a hand on Kay's shoulder. She brought her hand up and rested it on mine. "I'm so sorry for your loss. I do wish it'd been a different outcome."

There wasn't much of an exchange between Jack Henry and Kay.

"What was that?" Jack Henry was somewhat hostile after we'd gotten into the cruiser and down the road.

"That was a woman being sensitive to another woman during a time of grief." I simply stared ahead. "Grief doesn't know time, Jack."

Suddenly I just found myself so angry with him.

"You only see a crime. A crime that has to get solved. I see a little girl that's a ghost that's begging her mother to notice her. Playing with her hair and tickling her mom just to see her laugh. Then I see a mother who looks at me and sees the daughter she lost." I stopped myself from saying any more. "Listen, I'm sorry. I know I shouldn't bite your head off. But I'd lie if I didn't say that I'm upset you're still thinking about taking the state job. What am I going to do without you? That's two people I've lost in six months."

"Emma Lee, I love you. I'm not going anywhere. I'm still going to be your boyfriend. It's not like we're breaking up." He reached over and put his hand on my leg.

"It feels like I'm losing you." There was no way to sugarcoat it. "I can't imagine not seeing you every day."

"Let's not put the cart before the horse." He gave me a couple of pats before he stuck his hand back on the wheel as we made our way back to Sleepy Hollow.

Chapter Twelve

Since there were no calls for clients the next day at
Eternal Slumber, I figured I'd head back to the library and
check out the arson case. Somehow Betsy got to the barn
and if there was a connection, maybe I could connect the
dots.

"Twice in a week. Hmmm. . ." Mazie Watkins looked
up from the library reference desk with a curious eye.
"Twice in a lifetime." This time her brows rose.

"And I brought you a coffee." I walked over and
handed her the large special coffee from Higher Grounds.
"I hear the caramel salted latte is your favorite."

"Cheryl Lynne's a gossip." She took the drink and a
sip. "And the best barista around."

"Yes she is. And I've got a favor to ask." I leaned on
the counter of the reference desk.

"Hence the coffee," she muttered and brought the to-go
cup up to her mouth for a sip.

"I know that you have friends on the police force, so
I'm asking you to keep quiet about my snooping around the
newly reopened cold case." I carefully watched her
features.

She'd help out the department in research and even let
them have their monthly FOP meetings in the library
conference room.

"I did look up the history on the computer after you
left." She planted her elbows on her desk and held the cup
with both hands in front of her face. The steam from the
coffee curled up out of the little opening on the plastic

coffee top and fogged the front of her face. "I'm just curious how you knew to look up Betsy Lynn Brady before the case was even reopened."

"Jack Henry had gotten some tips and he was telling me about it. I figured I'd come here and see what I could figure out with the library database." Casually I took a drink of my coffee, almost convincing myself.

"Why do I need to keep it a secret that you're looking into it if someone asks?" she asked.

I knew better than to think she was just going to grant my favor of asking her to keep her mouth shut because she was newly inducted into the Auxiliary Women's Group, the one I busted into and the one Beulah Paige Bellefry was the President of. As long as she was in charge, there was no way she was going to include me. This was prime gossip for them. Even though it seemed harmless, it still gave them something to peck to death.

"I wouldn't want to compromise the police department and notify the killer, who's now lurking around to see if they're going to be caught." I made it sound really scary.

"Killer?" she asked and drew back. "I read that there was a fire set – as in arson. Are you saying the owner of the property is a killer because I didn't find anywhere that remotely made me think he knew about the little girl in there. Nor did I find anything that connected him to Kay Brady or her fancy fiancé." She quirked a brow.

"Wow." My jaw dropped, my brows rose. "Someone's been looking into this." My chin tilted to the side and I looked at her sideways. What was her angle?

"What?" Her shoulders lifted to her ears. "You had me curious. You never come to the library."

"True." I wasn't so good at the incognito stuff, but I was good at bribing. "So, I guess we can put our heads together and figure out some things about the fire."

She jumped up. With her coffee in one hand and the file in the other, she came over. She slid the papers across the counter of the reference desk to me.

"Herman Strauss owned the property. The company that bought it from him had in the contract that he had to take the barn down. Strauss is so cheap, he decided he'd set it on fire. The problem and reason he went to jail is because he was paid for the property and it was no longer his. Since it was owned by the company when he torched it, it was against the law." She had really researched the case.

"OSHA?" I asked about the regulatory laws.

"Yes." She nodded and took a sip before she continued. "That made it a federal law which Strauss didn't know. He was too cheap to keep up his end of the deal." She smacked the papers. "That's why he went to jail for arson. So when they announced they found bones in the charred barn yesterday, I started to think about the little girl you were looking up."

"Hmm." I had to really be more careful.

"He has no ties with her whatsoever." She took a step back and enjoyed some more sips of her coffee. "Betsy had to be playing in there, because according to the paper." She pulled up this morning's copy of the *Sleepy Hollow Gazette* where there was a photo of the barn before it was burnt down and a photo of Betsy with the headlines: *Cold Case Solved.*

Betsy appeared next to us. I smiled at her and then back at Mazie.

"Case solved." She pointed to the paper. "Says it right here."

"Can I keep these and look over them?" I asked knowing the case was far from solved.

"But it's over," she protested. "Unless you've got some information that hasn't been brought to light." She leaned closer and took her finger off the paper.

"Nope. I just want to read over everything myself." I shrugged and nonchalantly took a drink.

"Fine." She popped up to standing straight up and rolled her shoulders back. "And I won't say anything," she whispered when someone had walked into the building. "Especially if you send me a wedding invitation." She winked.

"Thanks, but I'm not engaged. Jack Henry has never asked me and I'm not sure where all the rumors came from." I pulled the file toward me and put the newspaper in it.

"Maybe it's because Zula Fae has been telling everyone and you know, you're going to be thirty."

I thanked her and took the file and decided not to even comment on the age thing. "I'm going to look around."

"Emma Lee Raines, are you becoming a reader?" There was a bit of excitement in her voice.

"Just looking around." I couldn't wait to see her face when she realized all her investigating was null and void when we did nab the person who deliberately killed Betsy.

There were really two investigations going on. Jack Henry's investigation into what happened to Betsy Lynn Brady, which we knew was murder because she was ghosting me, but he had to prove she was murdered before he could really nose around potential suspects. Then there was my investigation on who did kill her and bring the killer to justice.

The first person I thought I'd check out was Herman, the man who was put in jail for the arson charges and who owned the barn.

Betsy had moved over to the children's section of the library. She and Mr. Whiskers were curled up in the beanbag.

"My mommy didn't hurt me. But I'm glad she never married Kevin." Betsy rubbed down Mr. Whiskers's tail.

I grabbed one of the books that was opened like a tent on the top of the bookshelf next to the beanbag.

I pretended to read it out loud but spoke to Betsy, "What exactly happened between you and Kevin?"

"He didn't want children. He wanted to send me off to a school away from my mommy. I heard them yelling about it. And. . .," her voice cracked, "Mommy was thinking about it."

"Oh, honey, why do you say that?" I asked trying to comfort her. "Your mommy really loves you. She didn't even get married after you died."

"I don't know why they didn't get married, but he didn't like all the noise I made. I wanted to have my friends for a sleepover. When I did, he threw a glass up against the wall when he told my mommy to make us stop laughing. They were my friends. Even though he said it was going to be my home, he lied!" She thrust her fists into the beanbag and disappeared.

"In the initial investigation of Betsy's disappearance, the cops thought her mom put her in a facility to cover up the crime or that she'd plead insane." Mazie held up another file when I was walking out of the children's section.

"What?" I asked.

"You still didn't look into Betsy's disappearance," she said.

Maybe she wasn't as flighty as I thought she was.

"There was definitely some forced entry into Betsy's bedroom window, according to the original police report.

They interviewed the mom, fiancé, and the maid. You know, they never got married and he stayed in the house." She handed me the file.

I opened it and scanned the police report.

"How did you get all of these reports?" I asked.

"Who were you talking to in the children's section?" she shot back.

"Myself." I gave her my standard reply.

"You might think I'm stupid and couldn't get another job, but I'm pretty smart. Not only book smart, but I'm a good observer." There was a look on her face that I'd never seen on Mazie. It was steady and sure of herself. "There's no such thing as Funeral Trauma. I've looked it up, researched it and researched it more and more. Doc Clyde gave you that diagnosis because they think you're riding on the coo-coo train."

"Don't you think I know that?" I could feel my body starting to tense. Where was she going with this?

"And I also have been watching you. You've helped Jack Henry with investigations that no one had information on. Little details only the dead person would know. I've gone back and looked at his reports that no one else would even look at because they're just happy it's solved. Every time you've helped, it's been a murder." Her eyes darkened. "I'm fascinated with the paranormal and all things ESP. I think you've got the gift of seeing dead people."

I opened my mouth to protest. She put her hand up.

"Before you protest, I've looked it all up. You have the classic signs. Talking to yourself. Researching dead people. Getting the police to exhume bodies. Betsy Lynn Brady loved coming to the library and suddenly you show up here when you've never stepped a toe on the front step. Hell," she laughed, "I don't think you've ever walked in front of the library."

"Maybe you need to go see Doc Clyde." I brushed off her comments the best way I could but felt queasy that somehow I'd been so careless. "As for the investigations, for some reason I just have a knack."

"If that's what you want to call it." She smiled and her eyes narrowed. "But I can help you. I know things like getting into databases and things the layperson wouldn't know to do. Librarians do have access to several things, not just books."

"Yeah, well." I lifted the file up in the air. "Good to see you, Mazie."

Chapter Thirteen

The only other person who ever noticed my odd behavior that wasn't so odd was Jack Henry. Mazie was the first person who had asked if I could see dead people and I was sure my response seemed nervous and suspicious.

I couldn't get out of the library fast enough. I practically ran down the street and took a left down the sidewalk next to the square that led to Eternal Slumber. There were several questions I wanted to ask Betsy about the barn, if I could only keep her around long enough.

"Emma! Emma Lee! Over here!" Granny waved her arms from the gazebo in the middle of the square. Her hair was sticking straight up as though she'd just rolled out of bed. Her hot pink shimmering tights, orange off the shoulder shirt, and white headband was something Jane Fonda would've worn in her workout videos.

Mable Claire, Beulah Paige, and Hettie Bell were in downward dog, pushing up into pike position.

I hugged the file close to my body and walked across the street to say hello to them.

"Come on girls." Hettie encouraged them to keep going when I approached. "We aren't getting any younger."

"I'm going to take a break." Granny trotted down the steps. She was way more active than me. "Tell me, did Jack Henry hurry up with that ring after he saw the engagement party?"

"About that." I sat down on the step and she sat down next to me. "The ring that I thought was for me was really his mom's. He was picking it up from the jewelers for her."

The edges of my eyes burned with tears.

"Emma," Granny sat down, put her arm around me and laid her head on my shoulder. "Honey, I'm so sorry on so many levels. I shouldn't've had the party." She patted my leg and something flashed.

I looked down. Right there on Granny's ring finger was a ring.

"Granny!" I gasped and grabbed her hand. "Doc?"

"Mmm-hmm." She glowed. "He said that you might've had something to do with it. He said that when he saw how happy I was opening your gifts that he knew I was still on the market for a husband." She threw her head back and laughed. "I told him he was brave because I've outlived all my other men."

"Oh, Granny." Even though it seemed as if all the parts of my life were somewhat in limbo, Granny's life was coming together. "Are you happy?"

"I've always wanted to be a doctor's wife." She winked and held her hand out in front of her. "I've got to get my bridesmaids into shape." She nodded behind us. "Are you going to be my maid-of-honor?" she asked.

"Of course." I threw my arms around her and gave her a big hug. "Are you kidding me? This is going to be the wedding of the year."

"You can say that again." She fanned her hands out in front of her. "I can see it now. The entire day is going to be declared my day. I'm going to have an outside wedding right here. The chairs can go there and me and Doc will stand right up there with Pastor Brown behind us and you next to me." She pointed to the steps. "The girls will stand here. Each one on a different step. I've not decided if I'm inviting Bea Allen Burns or her nasty brother."

"Now, now." I *tsked*. "How could you even think of not letting them get so jealous of how amazing we are doing." I snugged her up real tight. "You're going to put on a pretty dress and smile to high heaven."

"I hope me and Doc make it to at least twenty years." She started to count on her fingers. "That'd put me damn near one hundred. I think I'll make it." She curled her nose. "I'm too mean to die."

"Twenty years." The number rolled around in my head. Twentieth anniversary. "Granny! You are a genius." I jumped up. "I've got to go, but I'll be over for supper tonight and you've got to tell me all about how Doc proposed."

Granny let out some ah's, huh's, and yeps, as I took off toward the funeral home. The morning was wasting away and Granny had given me a fabulous idea. There was no time to waste.

I hurried up the front steps of the funeral home and headed on inside to grab the keys to the hearse.

"Emma Lee, is that you?" Vernon Baxter called from the employee kitchen. The smell of fresh coffee drifted down the hall and hit me in the face as I approached my office.

"It is. I'm grabbing my keys. Hold on," I called back.

Next to my bag and the keys was a hand-written note from Jack Henry. He wrote that he'd stopped by because Cheryl told him I'd already been to Higher Grounds to pick up two coffees. He asked me to call him. He'd obviously thought the coffee was for him, which normally it'd be, but not today.

"How's it going?" I asked Vernon after I walked into the kitchen and stuck the file Mazie had given me into my bag.

He was pouring himself a cup of coffee and adding his sugar. Vernon was a very good-looking older man. He was sophisticated looking with his silver hair and steel blue eyes. I could only imagine the women he'd gotten in his younger days. Nowadays, he didn't seem to care about any relationship except with the corpses in the morgue.

"Disturbing." He offered me a cup of coffee. Interested in his words, I accepted.

"The case?" I asked and grabbed the creamer.

"Yes." He set his cup and my cup on the small café table before he pulled out my chair and his. He sat down. "I've got what looks to be two sets of bones. A skeletal cat."

As soon as he said that, Mr. Whiskers appeared and rubbed his body around Vernon's ankles. His tail curled around Vernon's pant leg.

"And the little girl. I got back her dental records and it's confirmed to be Betsy." Which I knew from Jack Henry, but I let Vernon continue, "The way the roof fell on her, it really didn't disturb her body. It looks like the barn beam had broken her back, the smoke had suffocated her and her cause of death was smoke inhalation. You think the little girl was playing in there with the cat, which Jack said she didn't have a cat, so we can safely assume it was an old barn cat."

"Mr. Whiskers isn't just any old barn cat." Betsy sat on the kitchen floor with a book in her lap. Mr. Whiskers scurried over to her. "He's my friend."

"It appeared as if the cat had curled on Betsy's face to shield her from the smoke. We obviously know the outcome. I wondered why her hands weren't up around her face as a common reaction would be to cover your own mouth and nose or run out, but I found this." He pulled out his phone and flipped to the photos. There were marks on the bones that weren't normal.

"Was she tied?" I asked.

"Yes. It appears as if she had her wrists tied together. The way the bones were found, her wrists were behind her hip bones." He let out a long sigh, eased back into the chair, and ran his finger along the rim of his coffee cup. "I'm afraid this was a homicide. Someone probably took the little girl, put her in the barn figuring it was safe."

"In a separate incident Herman Strauss was torching the place so he didn't have to pay someone to do it and that's how Betsy died." I thought for a moment. "But who would've put her there?"

Was it Kevin? Was it her mom? There was only one way to find out.

"I don't know who would've been so sick to do this to a little girl, but I do know that I've got to go see Herman Strauss. From what I understand, he's out of jail now." I patted my bag where I'd stuck the files. "In any case, I'm not so sure someone wanted the little girl dead as much as missing."

Mazie did a good job with her investigation.

"Hey." Vernon stopped me before I walked out of the kitchen. "I hear congratulations are in order."

"Can you believe it?" I knew he was talking about Jack Henry and the engagement rumor. "Granny is going to do it a third time. Poor Doc Clyde. Doesn't he know how her other husbands turned out?"

I left Vernon standing there speechless. Granny and Doc were the last couple on people's minds. At least it'd become a great way to deter any more rumors about Jack and me. Especially now that Jack was thinking of taking the state job.

I knew I was being a baby and I knew that I had to talk to him. Only I couldn't bring myself to do it just yet. I wanted to work on my Betweener job and that meant that I had to do it alone. Well, with Betsy's help.

When I got into the hearse, I pulled out Mazie's file where I'd seen Herman Strauss's address. I plugged it into the GPS on my phone and drove the hearse in that direction.

I'd checked my GPS as it took me out toward the river. It seemed as if Herman had decided that once he'd gotten out of jail, he wanted to live a quiet life. Out near the river was about as quiet as you could get. Maybe a few passing boats or fishermen, but other than that, it was a pretty nice and easy-going area.

The man on the tractor in the front field had pulled over and stopped when he noticed me driving on his driveway. He pulled his hat off and jumped down off the machine and walked toward me. I stopped before I made it up to the house because I'd seen him get off. There wasn't any sense in me pulling up to the house when the man I wanted to see was probably him.

'"Herman Strauss?" I called.

He patted his chest with both hands. He was older than the photo in the file. He'd lost most of his hair. The skin under his chin was sagging and there were wrinkles around his eyes.

"Am I dead?" He laughed.

"Oh that." I was so used to driving the hearse and everyone was used to seeing me drive the hearse, it never dawned on me that it might throw Herman off. "I'm Emma Lee Raines and I own and operate Eternal Slumber."

"That's the man voice that I remember from the barn, but he doesn't look like him." Betsy stood next to him and looked up. Like she did with all the adults, she peered at him intently.

"How can I help you?" he asked.

"The county morgue is in my funeral home and we'd gotten some bones from the barn. . ."

He stopped me, "There ain't nothing I can say to you that I didn't already tell the police. I don't know anything about that little girl. I did my time for the crime I committed. I didn't check the barn when I lit it up. Like I said, I'd checked the barn the night before and slept on what I needed to do."

"The police have already been out to see you?" I asked.

"Yep." He nodded and put his hat back on his head. He pulled something out of the chest pocket on his shirt. "Ross. Jack Ross, Sheriff."

"I'm not with the police. Can you tell me what you told him? We are doing an autopsy on the bones and want to make sure that what happened and what the bones are telling us corroborate." I knew I could get in all sorts of trouble for this, but I had to help Betsy.

"Like I told the sheriff. I did set the barn on fire because I didn't want to pay to have someone come take it down. Like I said in court, I didn't know I was breaking any laws. They'd not started to build the strip mall and no one was around. When that newspaper lady came snooping around here last night, I figured something was going on with the barn. Then I read it this morning in the paper. I had nothing to do with that little girl. I'd never seen her a day in my life. From what I can figure, she's a runaway because her mama was getting married and the little girl threw a fit."

Betsy didn't like that at all. She raised her foot in the air and stomped on the man's shoes.

"Owww," Herman reached down and rubbed his toe, before she took a kick to his shin. "What on earth?" He rubbed his shin.

"I'm no runaway." Betsy was spittin' mad. "Are you sure that's the man that came in and set the fire?"

"You have arthritis?" I didn't try to stop Betsy from beating up on Herman. He didn't seem to have any compassion for the situation, which to some extent I could understand since he'd spent the last twenty years in prison.

"They told me that my mommy was going to get rid of me anyway and I needed to go ahead and leave. But they took me." Betsy's head dropped before she ghosted away.

"No, I don't have no darned arthritis." He hobbled around in a circle like he was trying to walk it off.

Abduction? Why did someone want to abduct her? My mind kept going back to Kevin. He didn't want kids. He was wealthy. Did someone want something from him?

"Thank you for your time." I gestured to his tractor. "Sorry to interrupt."

"Like I said, I'm more than happy to cooperate, but I didn't do anything to any little girl." He shuffled on back toward the field.

"One more question." I turned around. "Are you sure you set the fire to your own barn?"

"Mrs. Raines." He stopped.

"Ms. Raines. Emma Lee," I corrected him.

"Emma Lee, don't go sticking your nose in places it doesn't belong." He turned back around and headed on back to his tractor.

"Betsy, are you here?" I asked once I'd gotten back into the hearse and on the road back to town.

If I was going to get any good leads, I needed to know exactly what she remembered, even just the pieces would help.

"If you come out and talk to me, I'll take you back to the library." Not that I was a mother or anything, but I'd heard my fair share of mothers bribing their children to be good during funerals. "I'll even read you whatever book you want me to read."

"Really? I love all the Dr. Seuss books. My mommy always read them to me." She appeared in the front seat. Mr. Whiskers sat next to her.

"You know," I smiled at them. "Mr. Whiskers really did try to save you. Do you remember that?"

"It's been a long time to remember anything." Her little eyes blinked. "My mommy sorta looks like my mommy, but sorta doesn't."

"Well, it's been almost twenty years. You'd be my age." I couldn't help but think what she'd look like today and if we'd crossed paths and been friends. I definitely wouldn't have wanted to be her friend if I was still ten.

"Twenty years," her voice faded.

"Do you remember anything about leaving your house for the last time?" I wasn't sure how to ask questions to a child without her getting upset.

"I remember looking back at the door. The outside light was still on and the house was so big, but once we got into the car and drove off, the house looked so small." She sighed. "I knew my mommy wasn't going to give me away. Why did I listen?"

"Who said that to you?" I asked.

"That girl. That little girl with long black hair." She finally gave me something that I could actually sink my teeth into.

"Do you remember the little girl's name?" I asked.

"It was different. Albertine." Betsy looked over at me with an element of surprise on her face. "She didn't tell me her name, but someone yelled Albertine when she tied me up."

Betsy used her small hand to rub her wrists.

"At first I thought she was joking because she was little like me. She tied me up with rope and it fell off when I moved my hands." She put her hands in the air as though she were showing me how she did it. "Someone said, 'Albertine, like we practiced.' And I continued to laugh because it was like a magic trick I was able to get out of."

"You thought she was kidding?" I asked.

"Yes. After a few tries, someone came in with a mask over their face. They weren't as nice as Albertine. They hurt me. And they were mean to Albertine." Betsy clasped her hands in her lap. "So now can we go to the library?"

"Yes. But first I need to make a stop. You might not like it." I pulled the hearse to the side of the road.

Kevin, Kay's fiancé, had been interviewed by the police and it seemed like he was a suspect, but for some reason he wasn't pursued.

"But you said we would go to the library," she whined.

"We are, but I have to go see Kevin first." I dug in my bag to retrieve the piece of paper Kay had written down Kevin's number and address on.

"No. Why? I don't want to." Betsy was sounding more like my child than a client.

"I know this is hard, but you wanted my help and that means that I have to talk to and see everyone who you knew. Even the ones that hurt you." I wasn't sure Kevin hurt her, but there was something that she didn't like about him.

"He didn't want children. He told my mommy." She sniffled. "He didn't want me."

Just like that, Betsy ghosted away.

Chapter Fourteen

Even with twenty years passed, the mansion that Kevin Allen owned was still by today's standards considered a mansion.

"If it looks this big from the road, imagine what it looks like inside," I mumbled to myself and looked out of my windshield at the massive house that sat way off the road.

I rolled down the hearse window and pushed the little black button on the silver box. It appeared it was the only way to get the gates to open.

"How can I help you?" the lady asked.

"I'm here to see Kevin Allen. I'm Emma Lee Raines from Eternal Slumber Funeral Home." I stated as if I had official business with him. "He wanted to see me about some pre-need funeral arrangements."

"Hold please," the person said and clicked off the speaker.

"All you have to do is push the button on the side of the box. That's what Momma would do when she forgot to take that button thingy that hangs up there." She pointed to the visor.

"I'm glad you are here. I really do need you and could really use your help." It was time for some more book talk. "Did you ever read Nancy Drew?"

"Oh, I love mysteries." She smiled real big.

"That's great because we have to pretend to be Nancy Drew and figure out how exactly you got to the barn and who took you." I nodded and reached my hand out to feel for the button. "Voila." I pushed it and the gates started to open.

"This is going to be a lot of fun. I love mysteries." Betsy bounced in her seat. When she looked forward the bouncing stopped. "I really hate that house."

"Really?" The closer we got the bigger the house was. "I'd think you'd like to have a big place to play and run around in."

"Why do mommies think that?" she asked. "When me and Mommy would go places, they'd always talk about how nice and big the house was. I think it's cold and lonely. But not when Lu came."

"Did Lu work here?" I questioned her.

"She lives here." Betsy laughed.

I put the hearse in park when I got up to the front of the circular drive. The main part of the house looked to be three stories tall. There was a small, enclosed breezeway to the right side that joined another two stories. The grass was nice and green, no doubt from the sprinkler system that was spitting away. The mums had already started to come up with pops of vibrant yellows, oranges, and reds. The pasture on the left side of the mansion had at least six horses, beyond that I could only see miles of farmland.

"There's a pool out back. If you like that sort of thing." Betsy's voice was calmer than it had been over the past few minutes. "My mommy really wanted to live here. She said that it would change our lives. She always told me to be a good girl."

"I bet you were always a good girl." I couldn't imagine she'd be anything else.

"Can I help you?" An older man with wire-rimmed glasses, short brown hair that was parted on the sides, a small pot-belly that hung over his khaki pants and snug against his short-sleeved golf shirt that was tucked in, pulled next to the hearse in a golf cart.

"Hi." Startled, I grabbed my Eternal Slumber *Welcome to Your Eternal Life* packet out of the glove box and got out of the car. "I'm here to see Kevin Allen."

"Is Mr. Allen dead?" The man chuckled.

"I hope not." I returned his goofy laugh. "Is he here?"

"Right here in the flesh." The man held out his arms. The familiar voice of his commercials was in this man's voice, but not his face. "Living flesh that is."

"That's not Mommy's Kevin." Betsy's ghost hid behind me. "That's an old man."

"Hi," I stuck my hand out. "I'm Emma Lee Raines from Eternal Slumber Funeral Home in Sleepy Hollow. My funeral home is also the county morgue and we've recently gotten a cold case related to someone from your past." There was no sense in sugarcoating anything.

Betsy had taken an interest in how he appeared to be now. Still tall, but much heavier and much older. I guessed in her mind, time had not changed when in reality everyone was much older.

"He sounds like jerk Kevin. That's what I called him. But he doesn't look like him." She floated up in the air and swooshed side-to-side.

"All of the sudden it got awfully windy." Kevin noticed the breeze my Betweener client was making around him by her sudden movements. "Let's go in and talk."

"You don't seem too surprised to see me." I noticed he'd not asked me to leave or how I'd gotten in.

"Nah." He walked up the front concrete steps of the mansion and opened the massive wooden door with the Tiffany glass panels. "Kay called me. She said they'd found Betsy's bones."

"You mean Kay warned you." Betsy snarled. "Emma Lee, I can't go in there. I can't."

When I took a step inside, Betsy wasn't with me and neither was Mr. Whiskers. The foyer led straight into an open family room. The floor was cement and large abstract paintings hung on the wall. No telling how much each one of them cost. My morgue was warmer than this place. No wonder Betsy didn't want to live here. It was like a museum.

I followed him out to the back deck that overlooked the pool Betsy had talked about and a putting green off to the right.

"How can I help you?" He put his hand out for me to sit down in one of the lounges.

Before I could even say anything, one of his employees came out with a tray of assorted drinks.

"Please, make yourself comfortable." His charm exuded from him, just like he'd done on the TV.

"No thanks." I waved the employee away. So did Kevin when the tray was offered to him. "Bones tell a lot of the story about Betsy's final hours. We. . ." I cleared my throat, "I'm here to help put the missing pieces together for the report. Can you tell me exactly what you remember the morning Betsy was reported missing?"

"Yes. I remember getting a phone call from Kay. She was frantic. Naturally, I thought she was upset about the wedding. Something with the cake, the caterer, the dress, you know." He rolled his eyes. "Women and weddings." He then rolled his hand and I noticed his lack of a wedding band. "I told her to calm down and call the police after the staff had looked all over for Betsy. She was nowhere to be found."

"Were you at the office when Kay called? And what time was that?" I asked.

"I was in the Chicago office. It was the soft opening and I'd left the night before. Rent A Room was going national. Chicago was our first box store out of Kentucky. I've told the police all of this." He lifted his nose in the air and took a deep breath. "Don't you love the smell of fall? It's coming. We can't stop time."

"I do love fall in Kentucky." No wonder the police didn't question him too much. My eyes drew in front of me and beyond the deck. There was an amazing pool that had more curves than Beulah Paige. There was a concrete swan in the middle that spit water out of its beak. "You have beautiful land here."

"Yes. It's not used much, but I do love it here." He looked beyond.

"What is that patch over there?" I pointed to the far right of the property. It was a little more overgrown and the statues that were in the patch looked like they'd fallen apart.

"I used to have a beautiful flower garden. There's a pond in there somewhere. The statues were also kept up." His voice held sadness. "Kay loved that garden. She and Betsy were in there every day doing something." The memory put a smile on his face. "After she left me, I didn't go back in there."

"Speaking of Betsy. Did you like her?"

"Of course I did. I mean, I loved Kay and she was part of Kay." He looked at me strangely. "I hope you don't think I had anything to do with Betsy's disappearing," he said all smarmy.

"No," I assured him. *Of course I do*, I pinched a smile. "I'm just trying to gather all the facts to go with the story her bones are telling me."

"And what are the bones saying nowadays?" He taunted me.

"Betsy was bound and gagged, making this a homicide. Someone killed her. Someone took her from your house and tied her up in that barn. Herman Strauss had no way of knowing Betsy was in there when he lit the place on fire."

"Geesh." His eyes dropped. "Does Kay know?"

"I'm assuming the police informed her." I didn't know for sure, but it was Vernon's job as coroner to inform the sheriff if there was something and homicide was a pretty big something.

"What was your relationship like with Betsy?" I asked and eased up on the edge of the seat. I couldn't help but notice him fidgeting.

"I was just her mother's boyfriend. You know she'd do the jealous thing like want her mom to herself and have her mom spend all her time with her." He shrugged.

"Like you wanted Kay's time and all her attention?" I asked.

"Yeah. I guess when you put it that way. But kids grow up. They move on and then leave their parents. That's all I told Kay." He shook his head. "I never wanted anything but the best for Betsy."

"So when you offered to send her off to school, that was a loving gesture for a ten year old?" Okay. My words might've been a little off-color as a guest in his house, but the facts were the facts. He didn't want children. He didn't want to compete for Kay's affection and he certainly wasn't the fun-loving Rent A Room king he portrayed on the TV.

"I think our little visit is over." He stood up. His sweet charm had turned cold and calculating. "If there is any further assistance needed, send the sheriff himself."

That jerk wasn't even going to show me the door.

"Wait a second," I called out after him. "You never married?"

"No. Not that it's any of your business." He walked inside and shut the door behind him. The sound of the lock let me know I wasn't using the way I came in to leave the mansion. That man didn't want me anywhere in his house.

That sent all sorts of red flags up to me.

"You can go around that way." Betsy stood at the top of the steps leading off the back porch.

There was no sense in hanging around here. I had more questions than answers. Doing more research on the great Rent A Room king was high on my priority list. Or should I say, Mazie Watkins's list.

I stood at the bottom of my steps and surveyed the quickest way around the massive structure. To the left were the fields and to the right was the right wing of the house and the way Betsy had gone. She'd lived here, so I took her way.

The breezeway that connected the two houses was glass on both sides. There was a shadow that caught my attention from the first window of the right wing. Being the nosy person I was—I had no idea why I tiptoed over to the window because Kevin knew I was there—I pushed up on the pads of my toes and looked in.

The room appeared to be the laundry room where a woman was folding laundry. She looked up and we stared at each other before I looked away and kept on walking.

"You there!" I cringed when I heard someone call after me. "Who are you?"

"Lu!" Betsy rushed over to the woman who'd been folding laundry. Both of them stood next to the door that led from the breezeway. Betsy was excited. "She was the only employee nice to me."

"Lu," I put my hand out to greet her. "Hi! Remember me?"

I didn't know how this was going to play out, but I needed someone from the inside on my side.

"No. I don't recall?" She eyed me suspiciously.

"I'm Betsy's friend. I came for a sleepover a few times. Sadly, I'm the undertaker of Eternal Slumber in Sleepy Hollow. We are also the home of the county morgue and the sheriff had us extract some bones they'd found in a barn." I looked down and tried to put a crack in my voice, "I came to tell Kevin that they were Betsy's bones." I did the sign of the cross like Granny always did, even though we didn't have an ounce of Catholic religion in our own bones.

Immediately, Lu did the sign of the cross and fell to her knees. She started to pray and lift her hands up to the sky.

"Do it!" Betsy coaxed me.

My eyes darted back and forth to see if anyone else was around. When I saw the coast was clear, I fell to my knees and put my hands in the air like Lu. When I tried to make out what she was saying, it dawned on me that she was speaking in Spanish.

She reached over and grabbed my hands, jerking it in two quick motions to the sky before she said a word I knew.

"Amen." She kissed her fingers. "Are you sure?"

"I'm positive." I could throw a good tear or two. It was something a good undertaker could do if needed. "I'm also sad to report that it appears that Betsy was killed. Murdered."

"Please stop being mean." Betsy looked up at me like I'd lost my mind.

Lu gasped. "No. No." She shook her head. "Who would harm such a sweet little girl?"

"I'm hoping to find that out." It was time for me to plant the little seed. "Not only because I was best friends with Betsy," I tried to read Lu's face when I said that to see if she bought it, "but also because I want to find out who did this senseless act to our friend." I reached out to offer a loving hand to Lu. "As a professional I have to find out who did this."

"Poor, poor, Kay." Lu glanced up at me from underneath her brows.

I couldn't be sure if she was buying my act of childhood friendship, but I felt like she was.

"Yes. Kay is devastated." A long deep sigh escaped my body. "She's taking it pretty hard. In fact, she's the one who told me I should come here and ask Kevin some questions."

"She did?" Lu drew back as if I'd just accused him of killing Betsy.

"She did," I confirmed. "I remember Betsy not liking him at all."

"But. . ." Betsy tried to interrupt me. I kept on talking.

"Yes. I remember Betsy saying that he wanted her gone. Wanted to send her off to school. Out of his hair so he could have Kay all to himself." Out of the corner of my eye, I could see Betsy ghost away.

"I never recalled a bad relationship between Kevin and Betsy. I remember him not wanting to have his own children, but I also remember very vividly all the toys he'd bring her back from his travels as well as the lavish parties he'd throw for her friends." Lu's eyes drew up and down me. "If you were such good friends with Betsy as you say you were, then you'd know about the parties."

I glanced around. Where did Betsy go? My mind raced. Had she lied to me? Had that little girl used her cute little ghost ways to make me feel sorry for her and not stay focused on the case? There was something fishy going on.

"It's hard to remember. It was twenty years ago." Why had Betsy remembered Lu when she couldn't remember anyone else?

Chapter Fifteen

The day was slipping by and with Betsy disappearing on me, there wasn't much I could do without asking her a few questions. I really wanted to try and get her to remember more about the day she was taken. There was a niggling feeling that Kevin was more involved than he wanted to or cared to admit.

There wasn't much more I could do until I talked to her, so I wanted to go see Granny before I hung out with Jack Henry for the night. I also wanted to tell her about how he was thinking about going to the state police. Knowing her, she'd give me some offbeat advice and I'd be wasting my time.

Instead of parking at the Sleepy Hollow Inn, I went ahead and parked the hearse at the funeral home and walked across the square. It was actually turning out to be a nice night that wasn't too cool. You could never tell about the seasons in Kentucky. One minute it was hot, the next minute it was cold and possibly snowing.

It was the strangest sight not seeing at least one of the Sleepy Hollow Inn's guests sitting in one of the rocking chairs. Granny provided a nice quilt that hung on the back of the rocker in case the guests got cold while rocking.

I walked up the steps and heard voices coming from inside. When I opened the screen door and walked in, I noticed the guests were in the gathering room and none too happy.

"What's going on?" I asked Hettie Bell.

"Your granny." Her right eyebrow rose. "She asked me about the juices I drink in the morning."

"Yeah?" I tried to look above the crowd and the rumbling of grumblings.

"She decided that she needs to fit into a different wedding dress and the only way to do that is to get all the snacks out of the gathering room," she said as calm as could be.

The crowd parted and in straight view was Granny. She was in a wedding dress that was too small for her and pinned with large safety pins. She held a glass of something green that looked as nasty as it would taste. There was a big leaf or some sort of garnish sticking out of it. She used it to slowly stir the concoction and moseyed her way over to me leaving the guests to check out the new juicer bar that she'd apparently put in place of her homemade sweet tea.

"Here." She shoved the glass in my face. "It'll jump start your metabolism. Since you aren't getting married before thirty," she leaned forward, "because your body changes after thirty, you're gonna need one of those every day."

"What is wrong with you?" I asked. "Why can't you be that cute little southern granny that makes cookies, reads books, knits, and goes to bed at a reasonable hour?"

"That sounds god-awful," she said with heavily rouged red lips. "What do you think of my new dress?"

The wedding dress was snow white. It was meant to be skin tight from the bosom to the hips and flare out. Granny's body type was not fitting into the dress.

"I think it doesn't fit." Lines creased in my forehead as my brows dipped. "I think you need a nice dress that will go with your age and your body type."

"Third time's a charm," she chirped and gulped down the drink.

"And you can't be giving people green juices just because you can't control your urges." I clapped my hands to get everyone's attention. "Hi," I put my hand in the air when the guests faced me. "I'll be right out with some cocktails, sweet tea and some snacks as you wait for your supper."

I grabbed Hettie Bell by the arm and dragged her down the hall with me, Granny nipping on my heels.

"Emma Lee Raines," she snapped at me. "You can't just come in here like a bull and take over. This here is my inn."

"This inn is your home and income. If you don't take care of your guests, you won't have any." I pushed myself through the door behind Hettie and grabbed the large pot to start the water to boil for the sweet iced tea Granny was known for. "Hettie, can you get together a few finger sandwiches with some pimento cheese and cut them into triangles."

She nodded and got to work.

"Now, what are you cooking for supper?" My brow cocked at Granny.

She stood there with a scowl on her face. I walked over to the hooks and grabbed an apron off the wall. I threw it at her.

"I don't want you to get anything on that dress because once supper is cooked and served, we are taking that thing back where you got it." I noted and grabbed the tea leaves and sugar jar.

"I got it from the new wedding boutique that opened up next to Burns Funeral." She told me something I'd not yet heard. "If you even had an inkling of getting married, you'd have heard about it."

"It is all the rage right now. I've heard so many people are dying to get married just so they can hire them." Hettie slapped the pimento cheese on the bread and spread it quickly. "Southern Roots."

"Huh?" I asked and used the big scoop to dig out the sugar. I'd never ever tried to count the calories in Granny's sweet tea, but I knew it was a lot.

"Southern Roots is the name of the boutique. They also have a planning consultant in there." Hettie used the knife to cut the specialty bread in triangles and place them on the serving trays and tiers Granny used before she lost her mind.

Out of the corner of my eye, Granny was checking on the pot roasts she'd put in all the ovens. I was at least glad to see that she'd done right by the guests and made some home cooking.

"What about some do-drop biscuits?" I asked and pulled the flour jar out when I put the sugar jar back.

Granny's eyes snapped when she looked at the jar. It was her subtle way of telling me she wasn't happy, but she knew I was right.

"So this is how it's gonna be?" I leaned a hip on the counter. "Does Doc Clyde know that you went on some juicing diet?" I started to throw questions at her. "This marriage isn't just about you. He likes you just the way you are. Sweet tea and the smell of cinnamon and all."

Granny didn't think I knew her little secret. She liked to sprinkle some cinnamon and sugar on her hair so when she bent over to talk to one of her suitors, she smelled like homemade cookies because she knew men loved her cooking.

"You're being a mean old biddy," she squawked and tried to contain a smile.

"I will be thirty in a couple of days." I laughed and it was contagious because she started to laugh too.

As the two of us went about getting supper ready for the guests and Hettie got them seated at the tables as well as other dinner guests from the community, I decided to tell her about Jack Henry and the bomb he'd dropped on me.

"Bomb?" Granny shook her head. "I'd call that a nuke."

"You're not making me feel any better." I checked the tea that I'd put in the refrigerator to be served with supper to see if it was cool enough to put in the glasses over ice.

Instead of a water glass, Granny served each diner a Mason jar glass of tea as well as another drink they'd prefer. When I told her that people liked to have water, she claimed I was sassing her with big city ways and to lower my standards since I was a country girl with roots that ran deep in the sweet tea community. I guess she knew what she was doing because everyone loved her tea.

"You think it's his mama?" Granny asked a great question. "'Cause if it is, you need to go down swingin'."

That was the thing with Granny. She was as southern as they come and as sweet as her tea, but she could chew you up in a minute and you'd thank her afterward because the way she did it was so nice that you didn't see it coming.

"I don't think so." I helped get the roasted potatoes and wilted lettuce into the bowls. Granny served everything family style. She claimed it was good for conversation and bringing people together. "He said that he only told me."

"Are you going to try to keep a relationship?" Granny asked the question that rolled around in my head, only when I heard it out loud it made my stomach hurt.

"I don't know how we can." The pain in my heart was so powerful, I had to rub my chest with my hand. "As it is now, we barely get to see each other."

"Not that I think you should break up, but the old saying is true." Granny pulled the serving forks out of one of the clay crocks she kept on the counter and stuck one in each of the pot roasts. "You know the one about letting go and if it comes back it was meant to be."

"Yeah. I know," I muttered.

I also knew that I've loved Jack Henry Ross for as long as I could remember.

"Well, you go on." Granny came over and gave me a much needed hug. "It seems like you've got things to do other than sit here and look at this silly old woman in a too tight wedding dress."

I shook my finger at her.

"We are going to take that dress back. Shame on them for letting you buy it." I *tsked*, gave her a kiss and a hug before I headed back out the door.

I'd spent more time at the inn than I'd expected. I certainly had no plans of helping cook or even getting things back together so she'd not lose all of her guests, but I loved Granny. Crazy or not.

Jack Henry's cruiser was already parked in the back of Eternal Slumber. The side door to my efficiency was unlocked and I found Jack Henry in the small TV room to the left.

"Hey." I walked into the room.

He clicked the remote control and turned the TV off.

"Sorry I'm late. Granny nearly took her entire business down with one juice." I shook my head before I bent down and kissed him on the head. "Literally."

"What?" He laughed.

"You know that she and Doc Clyde are getting hitched," I called over my shoulder on my way across the hall to my bedroom. "There's a new wedding type boutique next to Burns and she went there."

I opened the door to my closet and pulled out my little black dress. It'd only take a few minutes for me to get changed and comb a brush through my hair to get ready for my supper date with Jack.

"She decided she wanted to wear a dress that was at least two sizes too small for her and she decided she wanted to juice to lose weight." I stood in front of the mirror in my small bathroom and tugged the dress in the appropriate places. The brush glided through my hair and I swiped some red lipstick on to add a little color to my face. "She insists she can't do it with all the snacks she has in the gathering room and the sweet tea."

I grabbed the pair of hoop earrings off my dresser and walked out, putting them in.

I continued my story.

"She replaced the tea bar with a juicer bar." I laughed and stared at my handsome boyfriend.

"I hope you are as feisty as she is when you're her age." He stood up from the couch and looked at me. There was a silence that hung over both of us and we knew what it was.

"Does that mean you've made your decision and you're not going to go because you definitely want to keep this up." I gestured between us. "And you don't want any time or space between us?"

"Is that what you want?" He walked over to me. "God, you are beautiful."

There was a sound in his voice that told me he'd made his decision and it wasn't one I wanted to hear.

"You're going to take the job, aren't you?" I gulped back the flood of tears that were building up in my eyes.

"Emma Lee." He lifted his hand to my face and tucked a piece of hair behind my ear. "Don't cry. There's nothing to cry about."

"You're moving." My lips were so dry. I curled them into my mouth and raked them across the top edge of my teeth. A tear fell down my face. He brushed it away.

"I'm not moving for long." He ran his hand down my arm. "When I met with them again today, they could tell I was apprehensive, so they offered me a temporary position for six months. We can do six months apart. It's not like I won't see you."

"I know you. You'll throw yourself into your work and your intentions might be good but. . ." I couldn't do what Granny had suggested I do.

The thought of telling him to go and see if he came back was like I was letting go of a grenade. Once I let him go, it would explode. It took me at least fifteen years to get him, now I just couldn't let him go that easy.

"You've not been present the past months anyways." He squeezed me to him. "You can take the next few months and deal with Charlotte's death without putting on a brave face for me. I want to be here for you in your grief but you won't let me."

As much as it hurt to hear, he was right. I'd not dealt with Charlotte's death the way I should and I probably did need some time. But not time without Jack Henry.

"I can get help with you here." I could hear my begging.

"You need to focus on you. Then I want you to focus on me." His breath was warm on the top of my head. He hugged me tighter. "I want you to focus on us like you did before Charlotte died. It will be good for you even though it doesn't seem like it now."

It completely dawned on me.

"Are you doing the whole let it go and if it's meant to be it'll come back?" I pulled away and looked at him.

"What are you talking about?" Confusion was all over his face.

"Nothing." My paranoid state was taking over. Now I didn't feel like he loved me and he was breaking up with me. "Are we breaking up?"

"No," he said. "No," he reiterated.

"It sure feels like it." The tears flowed down my face and I suddenly didn't feel much like going out.

"We are still an us. And I'm still going to be your contact for your Betweener clients." His voice cracked. There was a hurt on his face. More like an uncertainty.

My eyes drifted into the TV room. Betsy and Mr. Whiskers stood in the dark corner. Even with Jack Henry there and my Betweener clients, I'd never felt more alone.

Chapter Sixteen

"My, oh, my." Mazie *tsked* behind the reference desk. "Three times in a week."

She was right. I'd never stepped foot in the library three times in my life, much less three times in a week.

"And so early." She looked me up and down. "No coffee?"

"Are we alone?" I'd deliberately planned to be here early. Just not this early.

Last night after Jack Henry and I talked a little bit longer, we'd gotten take out and sat in front of the TV. Neither of us wanted to go out anymore. We'd decided we just wanted to spend time together until it was time for him to leave for his six-month stint with the state. Though he'd stayed over and we had a connection like we'd never had, I was starting to feel a disconnect. More than likely it was me that was putting the distance between my heart and reality so I could cope better. It was something to explore but not now. Now I had to get Betsy's case solved and get her crossed over.

"We are alone." Her face softened, her eyes squinted in coordination with the slow, easy smile that tipped the corner of her lips. "You have something to tell me, don't you?"

It might be something I regretted, but in my gut it seemed like the right thing to do.

"Mazie, you and I've never been great friends. We're friends and we've never had our differences and this might be something to bring us a lot closer." I tapped my finger on the counter and took a deep breath. "Like a band aid," I whispered, "rip it off."

"You are a medium," she gasped in delight.

"Not necessarily." I made sure to watch her reaction. "Before I tell you anything, I need you to promise me that you won't say a word and if you do, I'll deny it until I die."

"I'd never tell." She leaned forward. Her eyes were twinkling.

"I'm only telling you because I feel like you are a source of knowledge and up until now," I swallowed the lump in my throat, "Jack Henry has always helped me. He's going to be taking a temporary job with the state police and I'm going to need someone on my side."

"And you picked me?" She squealed with excitement.

"I picked you only because you are more in tuned to me and what's going on. I'm not sure why, but you are." I sucked in a deep breath. "I'm what you call a Betweener. I found out after that Santa over Artie's Meat and Deli fell on me."

She snapped before she pointed at me. Her jaw dropped and her eyes grew big.

"I remember that. I didn't put two and two together and realize it was then that Doc Clyde diagnosed you with the bogus disease." She nodded her head back and forth like a turtle. "So the hit on the head did it?"

"Yes. When I woke up, Ruthie Sue Payne was standing next to me with Chicken Teater." My lips pinched, as did my brows. "It's not just anyone who dies. It's only those who have been murdered."

It looked as if Mazie was trying to say something, because her mouth had dropped wide open.

My phone chirped from my back pocket. It was Granny. She and Doc were at Eternal Slumber and needed to talk to me. I quickly texted her back since Mazie was trying to get herself together from my news and let her know that I was going to at least be another thirty minutes.

"Wait." Mazie stuck her hand out. She'd obviously been playing the last couple of years of crime in her head. "Are you and Jack Henry really an item or have you just been working for him as the informant?"

"Initially, he was like you. He knew there was something going on with me. I felt like I could trust him, like I feel like I can trust you." I watched her face. It seemed as though she was really touched by my trusting her. "Then over time, we grew into more than an informant type relationship into a real love."

The sting of a good cry grew from the tingling in my nose to the lids of my eyes.

"Since Jack is going to be going to the state police for a few months, I feel like I need someone who is smart and intelligent and can keep a good secret." I was talking about her.

"So all the people you've been helping him with that were murdered had come to you?" She was still trying to wrap her head around my Betweener gift.

"Yes. All of them. And now Betsy and Mr. Whiskers, a cat." It sounded like I was crazy.

"A cat?" she asked and started to nod her head. "I'd heard you'd been buying some cat food at the Buy and Fly."

"Yeah. News travels fast around here. I was trying to get the cat to come to me and trying different cat foods was my thinking. Little did I realize that he was with Betsy when she died." Which brought me back to my current situation. "Are you going to help me with Betsy or not?"

"I'm going to be your new partner?" She lifted her hand to her chest.

"I'm going to need someone to help me when Jack leaves." I put my hand out. "Can I trust you?"

"Absolutely." She took my hand and we gave one big shake. "What do you need from me?"

"I've only got about ten minutes until I have to go meet Granny at the funeral home, so here's what I know." I began to tell her about Betsy.

"Okay. I'm going to have to write all of this down like they do in the movies." Her voice grew excited.

"Movies? I thought you were a reader?" I questioned.

She stared at me, not entertained by my observation.

"I've been watching too, like Jack did. I've noticed your strange behavior. Your shifty eyes, darting in and out of rooms, looking off into space, twitches of the mouth as if you were talking to someone under your breath and your subtle finger movements." She'd said everything I'd been trying to do on the down low but obviously not very well.

"Was I that obvious?" I asked.

"No. Not from what I could tell. Trust me." Her voice escalated, "I watched everyone around you. What clued me in was the bogus diagnosis. Of course being a librarian, I was so curious and tried to Google and find things on Funeral Trauma and found nothing."

Suddenly she gasped.

"What?" I looked around to see what was going on.

"Did Charlotte…" her voice trailed off.

"Yes." I pinched my lips together to try and prevent the sting in my eyes from forming tears. "That's been the hardest. That and the fact there was a ghost attached to Betsy. She had even convinced Betsy that she could help her get to the other side. Then I realized the older person was a ghost."

"I read something about that." She turned and patted around the reference desk like she was looking for something. "Sometimes ghosts attach to other ghosts if they have something in common."

"In common?" I asked. "Betsy is clearly a child, but this woman was older."

"Do you remember her name?" Mazie continued to look around. "Maybe I can check into all my contacts for her too. They have to be related or the crime has to be related."

"I don't recall her ever telling me her name. She didn't stay around long. Betsy is the only one who has, but I'll ask her when I see her." I looked at the door when it creaked open.

"Hi!" Mazie called and waved at the mother and child that walked in. "Story time will be in a little bit."

The child jerked his hand from his mom and scurried in the direction of the children's section.

"You're busy and I've got to see Granny." I spoke a little softer when I noticed a few more mother/children combos came in. "Why don't you meet me at Eternal Slumber when you get a break?"

"What about lunch? Part-time help comes around lunch and I can get away then." She smiled. There was definitely excitement in her voice and the bounce in her step when she came out from behind the reference desk was a good indication too.

"I'll see you at lunch." I waved her off and when I got to the door, I held it open for another group of mothers and their children.

The smell of coffee was carried in the morning breeze. It was like magic and I'd completely forgotten to go see Granny. Like a lost leaf, I floated down to Higher Grounds, which was packed. The small café tables were filled. I darted in and out between them and especially the one that was filled with Beulah Paige, Mable Claire, and Bea Allen Burns.

"Can't you do anything with Zula Fae?" Beulah Paige didn't waste any time grabbing my attention when she saw me.

"Good morning, ladies." I nodded at Beulah and Mable. "Bea." I greeted with a flat voice and a raised brow.

"Mmm-hmmm." Her nose curled and her lips snarled. "I've got to go. I'm so busy at the funeral home."

"Yep. Me too. Gotta go." I knew Bea Allen had gotten down and dirty after running a pre-arrangements special of buy one get one half-off.

"Really?" Bea Allen gave me the stank eye. "From what I hear, you don't even got a warm body waiting for you."

There was a time I'd have shot back at Bea Allen and that time was when Eternal Slumber was overflowing with bodies. Some people were hesitant to make arrangements with someone who had been diagnosed with the Funeral Trauma. Not that I didn't know how to do my job, I did. It was that some didn't trust in me to handle their physical body at the end of the life.

"What? No smart aleck comeback?" Bea Allen's lip curled up as if she'd gotten my goat.

"I'm not going to respond to petty gossip that's not true." I turned back to tell Beulah and Mable goodbye.

"What about Zula?" Mable asked. "She told me that I had to go on a diet if I wanted to be a bridesmaid. Die in diet. No thank you." She nodded toward Beulah. "I'm having hard enough time staying on this side of the ever after, much less die-ette."

"Mmm-hmmm." Beulah brought a piece of her muffin up to her lips and popped it in. "You stand your ground."

Stand your ground. It took everything in me not to laugh. Neither of them would dare say that to Granny.

"Emma." Cheryl held a cup of to-go coffee up in the air and set it down on the counter after we made eye contact.

"Thanks!" I was lucky that she'd turned out to be so sweet and not make me wait in the line. Especially after I'd just remembered that Granny was waiting for me.

With the fresh cup of coffee in my hand and Betsy walking down the street next to me, I picked up the pace in my step down the sidewalk. It was only a couple of minutes walk from Higher Grounds and I could see that Granny's moped was chained up to the tree in the front yard of the funeral home.

I brought the coffee up to my mouth to hide my lips, "Betsy, do you remember the lady that was with you when you first came to talk to me?"

Her chin lifted up and down as she skipped down the sidewalk next to me.

"Do you remember her name?" I asked. "It's really important."

"I don't." She abruptly stopped in front of me and I stopped in my tracks practically dropping my coffee. "But she said that she was sorry. She always told me she was sorry and that she'd never leave me again."

"Again?" I chewed on the inside of my cheek.

"Huh?" Hettie Bell stood out in front of Pose and Relax with a chalkboard sign that had the times of her classes today. "Again what?"

"Again, all of your classes," I lied. I'd gotten good at that over the past couple of years. Or at least I'd thought I'd gotten good until Mazie had just cut me down. "How on earth do you do this job and keep up with Granny?"

Hettie laughed and took the moment to bend down and stretch.

"Thanks for stepping in yesterday. I love your Granny, but I'm not to the point where I can tell her what's what." She was in some sort of contortion position that I'd never be able to recover from even if she twisted me up in it.

"Speaking of Granny. She's at my office waiting on me." I waved and headed next door to Eternal Slumber.

On the way back to my office, I slipped the heat up on the HVAC. The afternoon was turning colder than I'd expected. It was bad enough for people to have a reason to visit a funeral home, the least I could do is make it warm.

"Granny, I'm sorry I'm late." I headed into the office. "Doc." I was taken by surprise when I saw Doc with her. "What do I owe the pleasure?"

"As you know," Doc Clyde spoke up. "I asked Zula to be my bride. I'm ashamed to say that after all these years, I've been a Burns client and I'd like to switch my funeral needs."

"Not that he's sick or anything." Granny dragged her fingernail from his shoulder down his arm to his hand, giving me the ewws. I think I even snarled. "Trust me, he's not." She wiggled her brows and leaned over giving him a long kiss on his lips.

"Alright." I rolled my eyes. "That's enough."

"What? We are going to be newlyweds." Granny winked and shimmied her shoulders.

I shuddered with the memory of how coo-coo she was over Earl Way Payne when she hooked him. Mainly she acted like a teenager in love to get at Ruthie Sue Payne, Earl Way's ex-wife, but ended up really loving him.

"Are you sure you want to marry this woman?" I laughed.

Doc Clyde glowed and said a resounding, "Yes."

"Well, I'll be more than happy to give you the family discount and even go as far as calling Bea Allen myself." It was something I was going to look forward to.

"Emma Lee!" Mazie busted through the door. "I've got a name." She was waving some papers in the air. "Oh. I'm sorry. I had no idea you were with your granny." She planted a fake smile across her face. "Zula, how are you?" Mazie's sweet southern voice did a good job covering up of the reason she was here.

"Fit as a fiddle, but we've wasted enough time here waiting on Emma Lee. We have errands to run for our wedding."

When the coast was clear, Mazie rushed over.

"Look here." She put the papers on the desk and pointed to the article headline.

"What's up with you two?" Granny appeared from around the office door.

Mazie and I jumped around with our hineys against the edge of the desk hiding the papers.

"Nothing." Mazie smiled. "Just two old friends talking about books."

"Mazie, I've found puddles deeper than you and this supposed friendship. I've never seen the two of y'all hanging out." Granny's eyes lowered. She looked between us with suspicion on her face.

"What can I say? I'm going to have some free time on my hands while Jack goes to work for the state police for six months. I figured I'd join Mazie's book club," I lied again.

"Book club?" Granny perked right on up like a daisy. "I love a good book club. Count me in!" She tapped the door. "Emma Lee, you pick me up after lunch and we'll head on over to Southern Roots." She turned and left.

"Book club?" Mazie drew back. "I didn't invite you to my book club."

"I know you didn't and I didn't invite you here until later. So this." I pointed between us. "And our little adventure," I leaned in and whispered, "has got to be the biggest secret of your life."

"Fine. You can come to my book club." She shook her head. "What did she mean about Southern Roots?"

"Granny and Doc you know are getting hitched." I let out an exhausting sigh. It'd become the way my body processed the stress that came with talking about Granny. "She went out and bought this beautiful wedding dress that's entirely too small for her."

"Oh no." Mazie laughed out loud.

"She had it pinned on her yesterday when I went over to see her at the inn. Needless to say," I couldn't stop laughing from the images I had in my head of Granny and that dress, "she needs to get her money back and I'm going to take her."

"You're going to love it there. I'm a consultant for them," Mazie said.

"A consultant?" I asked.

"Yes. All things bridal and weddings. I'm a pretty good party planner too." She nodded with confidence. "So I've been helping out a lot." She picked up the papers and held it out. "Let's get back to this."

I held my finger up and walked over to the office door. I looked down the hall to make sure Granny had really left and shut the door for good measure. The sound of the clicking latch on the door knob echoed off the wood-paneled walls of my office.

"Is it safe?" Mazie asked. I nodded and took the paper, doing a quick scan.

"This Rachael Bemis is missing? And she worked for Rent A Room in Chicago?" I dropped the paper down.

"Yes. Kevin was interviewed by the police there. The police questioned him on both cases at the same time. She still hasn't been found." She flipped to another page. "This is Rachael Bemis. Is this the ghost that was with Betsy?"

I didn't have to look at the photo too long to know that it was.

"Yes. In ghost form, they are a little more faded and less vibrant." I glanced over in the corner at Betsy. She'd been sitting cross-legged with Mr. Whiskers curled in her lap as she read her book. "Kinda in a state of worry. Not sure here or there."

"Is she there? Betsy?" Mazie's eyes drew over to the corner.

"She is. I need to get a book from you because I promised I'd read to her." My words caused Betsy to look up at me. I turned the photo of Rachael to face her. "Betsy, is this the lady that was with you?"

"Yes!" She ghosted over to me. "That's her. She's very sorry."

"Sorry for what?" I asked.

Betsy shrugged before she bent down and picked up Mr. Whiskers. He didn't seem to mind that his back end was dangling down as she gripped him around his front armpits and kissed his head.

"She keeps saying that this ghost is sorry but isn't sure why." Then it hit me. "Do you think that Rachael had something on Kevin and she knew he'd done something to Betsy. He killed her too."

"Remember that Kevin didn't kill Betsy. The smoke from the fire that Herman Strauss set killed her. Someone put her there and the more I think about it, the more I wonder if she was kidnapped, put in there but the kidnapper didn't know the history of what was going on at the property. Herman Strauss had no idea Betsy was in there and lit the place on fire." Mazie's mind was going a mile-a-minute along with her mouth.

"You might have something. But Kevin wasn't in town when Betsy was taken from her room." I reminded her.

"No, but she was in the mansion." She sucked in a breath.

Both of us stood there like we were stumped.

"I have read that killers sometimes come back to the scene of the crime." A slow smiled eased on Mazie's face into a big all-out grin. "Tomorrow is the twenty year anniversary."

And my thirtieth birthday I wanted to say, but didn't.

"What if we go see Betsy's mom and ask her to hold a vigil with balloons that light up. You've seen those, right?" Her brows furrowed. "Anyway, I'll take pictures all night of the people and we can ask Betsy if she recognizes any of them."

"What sicko comes back to the scene?" I couldn't wrap my head around it. "Though you might have a good idea."

"It's a great idea." Mazie picked up the receiver on my desk phone and jabbed it toward me. "Go on. Call her."

It didn't take that much coaxing and before I knew it, Mazie and I were in the hearse barreling toward Betsy's mom's house.

"I've never thought about having a real funeral." Kay sat at her table looking a lot more frazzled than she had when Jack Henry and I had gone to see her.

"I'm more than happy to provide Eternal Slumber for the funeral for free." It was the least I could do since it appeared Kay wasn't in any financial situation to have a real funeral for her daughter. I'd grown fond of the little girl and I wanted to see her have a good send off.

"I think the balloons would be so amazing going up in the town square of Sleepy Hollow with the back drop of the mountains just as the sun is setting." Mazie painted such a pretty picture that she had me convinced.

"I don't know." Kay was not as convinced. "Betsy never went to the square or to Sleepy Hollow for that matter."

I wanted to protest that it's exactly where she'd found me, but I didn't.

"My funeral home is right across the street from the square and she was found in the barn behind the old strip mall." I had somewhat of a logical thought.

"I'm a party planner. So I'm more than happy to quickly get this twenty-year vigil together. Emma's granny would love to do some refreshments." Mazie continued to volunteer people without asking them. "It's all settled. You just have to show up."

"Well then. . ." Kay wasn't sure what to say. "I guess it'll be fine."

"Ask her about that lady that keeps telling me she's sorry." Betsy climbed up in her mother's lap and twirled a strand of Kay's hair around her little finger.

"Do you know a woman by the name of Rachael Bemis?" I asked.

Kay reached up and scratched the side of her neck where Betsy had touched. It was as if she could feel Betsy.

"The name doesn't ring a bell." She shrugged. "You know, I feel Betsy here. I've never really felt her so close, so I'm definitely happy to have the vigil in her honor at the square in Sleepy Hollow."

"It's settled then." Mazie stood up. "All you need to do is be at the square by seven."

While Mazie finalized a few more details about what she thought we'd do at the vigil, I couldn't help but wonder how Kay didn't even ask who Rachael was. She'd completely changed the subject. Though I never thought Kay could hurt her child, I also couldn't dismiss the feeling she knew Rachael or at least had heard her name before.

"Where did you go in there?" Mazie asked once we got back on the road.

"I couldn't help but notice how Kay had skimmed over Rachael Bemis's name when I brought it up." I noodled on the thought. "Betsy is so different from other Betweener clients because she's a little girl and had not lived a full life like the rest of my clients. She doesn't really understand the process."

"The process?" Mazie asked. She held her phone in her hand.

"The idea that someone is going to have to go to jail. No matter who it is." My own words haunted me. "There doesn't seem to be a clear motive or suspect here."

"She can't tell you anything about the person?" Mazie was scrolling through her phone.

"No. She continued to say that the person would say something about her mom getting rid of her. That makes me think it had to be someone on the inside." I shook my head, hoping the jumbled up thoughts might makes some sense.

"Oh!" Mazie screamed out. "I've got a lead on Rachael Bemis."

"What?" Maybe Rachael was a key to the investigation that the police hadn't connected.

"Rachael Bemis was never found. Her family knew she was having an affair with someone but she never told them who. It looks like Rachael's daughter is still alive and I have a number." She held her phone in the air. "I'm calling."

"What are you going to say?" I asked. "You can't just call and say, hey, I'm looking into your mom's death. Because they don't know she's dead."

"No but I do." The voice coming from the back of the hearse made me veer off the road.

I jerked the wheel, careful not to overcorrect.

"Fine. I won't call." Mazie's nails were planted in the dashboard. Her phone had fallen on the floorboard between her legs.

Rachael Bemis stared back at me in the rear-view mirror. Her pointer finger rubbed the middle of her chest.

"Rachael." My mouth dried. "Glad you can join me. Us."

"She's. . ." Mazie's eyes grew big. Slowly her chin turned toward her left shoulder and eventually her eyes were looking behind her. "Get out."

"Right here, book nerd." Rachael appeared to be a bit of a snarky ghost.

I laughed. "That's not nice when we are trying to help you."

"Help me? I'm glad I'm dead. Or I'd have been in jail for kidnapping Betsy Lynn Brady."

That time, Mazie and I nearly went through the windshield after I slammed on the brakes.

Chapter Seventeen

"That's it." Mazie jumped out of the hearse and stomped her foot. "Move over!" She swung her finger out in front of her. "I'm driving us back to Sleepy Hollow. That's twice you've nearly killed me."

"I'm fine." I gulped for air. "Get back in before someone comes barreling around the curve and hits us."

"No. Not until you scoot over and do all the talking you need to do to . .. to. .." Frustrated, she gestured to the back of the hearse. "You know what I mean."

"Fine. But you aren't going to like what I've got to tell you." I scooted over to the passenger side and watched as Mazie ran around to the driver's side to get in.

"What did she say?" Mazie wasted no time in throwing the hearse in gear.

"She said that she's the one who kidnapped Betsy." I looked in the back of the hearse.

Rachael Bemis had lain on the empty church cart with her arms crossed.

"I've always wondered what this felt like since it never happened to me." She sounded a little jovial. "So what is it you want to know?" She sat up. Her legs straight out in front of her.

"First off, why did you take Betsy?" I asked.

"Oh, oh." Mazie sounded like a monkey. "Ask her if Kevin told her to do it?"

"You can ask her yourself because she can hear you and see you. You just can't see or hear her." I was going to have to get used to training Mazie.

"Kevin had been spending a lot of time in Chicago to open the new store. Long days led into late nights that ended in several cocktails every time he came to town." She smiled with a sexy look on her face. "He was so good looking. He was rich and I was a good listener. He told me how he didn't really want kids but had committed himself to that frumpy mother."

"Kay Brady?" I asked.

"What about her?" Mazie chirped in.

"Mazie, shh." I admonished her. "I'll tell you everything once I get the answers. That's how this partnership goes. Got it?"

Mazie took a hand off the steering wheel and zipped her fingers across her lips.

"Yes. Kay Brady." Rachael had a disgusted look on her face. She crossed her arms. "It wasn't that he didn't love Betsy, he did. He said that she was a sweet little girl and what's her name." She rolled her wrist in the air before she drew her finger back down to her chest and rubbed that same spot.

"Kay."

"Yeah. Kay." Her brow twitched. "He said that she had really done a great job raising her, but he wanted to be married and made first priority not second. He'd even brought Betsy to Chicago one time to go to the American Girl Store. I might've paid my friend to let me take her daughter and we ran into each other there."

"Did you and Kevin have an affair?" As a Betweener I'd seen this before. Another thing, people kill for no good reason.

"We slept together once. He said it was a mistake. I begged him to stay. I told him that I didn't have any children that were small." A sadness swept over her. "I did have two children and I sold them out."

"Huh?" I wasn't following her.

"I gave them to my mother to raise because I wanted Kevin to love me. He passed me by and had the store manager fire me before the store even opened." She fiddled with her fingers. "I'd become obsessed. I knew Kevin's schedule since I was the closest to him. I'd even had taken his keys while he was in Chicago. He thought he'd left them back in Kentucky so I had all the keys to his house. I took a train from Chicago to Lexington. It was then that I stalked Kevin and what's her name."

"Kay." I would continue to make her hear the name. It wasn't fair that she wouldn't recognize how she wronged someone.

"Stop saying her name." Rachael put her hands up to her ears and shook her head back and forth.

"I'll stop." I had to keep my cool because I couldn't take the chance that she'd ghost away. And I had to have a full story to end this.

"Don't be mad at me." She looked at me. "It was only to scare Kay and make her think that Kevin's house wasn't safe and dump him." She started to tear up. "Even though I hate what's her name."

"Ka . . ." I started to say but stopped myself when she glared at me.

"Betsy is a sweet little girl. I was simply going to just put her in this barn. Give her all the books she wanted and feed her. I had no idea it was being torn down. There was Mr. Whiskers and it was just awful." Her chin lifted high in the air and with her eyes closed she took several deep breaths.

"Why do you keep saying Kay?" Mazie asked.

"That's it!" Rachael's face dropped. "I'm sick of hearing her name."

Just like that, she ghosted away.

Chapter Eighteen

Even with seven or eight Betweener clients under my belt, none of them were a bit similar. I'd learned more and more as I'd gotten them. At first I thought I could only see murdered clients that I knew. Then it turned into murdered victims from the community that I didn't know. Now it had expanded even to people who'd been dead a long time that had nothing to do with my community or me.

"Rachael kidnapped Betsy. Herman had no idea Betsy was in there." Mazie was using Charlotte's old office in Eternal Slumber as a fact gathering space for our new collaboration. She'd taken an old white board that Charlotte had kept in her office from when we'd done the remodel and wrote suspect and motives on top of it with one of the dry-erase markers.

She listed Kevin and Rachael as the number one and number two. Under their names, she wrote why she felt like they had motive. Between them she drew a big heart and wrote affair in the middle.

"This gives Rachael motive." She tapped the heart with the felt tip of the marker.

"But who killed Rachael?" I asked.

"Kevin." Mazie sounded confident. "When the cops gave him a lie detector, he didn't kill Betsy. He killed Rachael."

"Where is her body?" I asked.

"Ask her." Mazie made a continuous circle around Kevin's name. "How does this work? Betsy and Rachael both hang around you until the killer is found?"

"That's the way it's been with my Betweener clients, but Betsy and Rachael are the first from out of our town that came to me." None of it was making sense.

"Can you hand me my phone?" Mazie stood looking at the board. "We've got to get the vigil together."

"Who are you calling?" I asked and picked up her phone off of Charlotte's desk and handed it to her.

"I'm going to call Rachael's daughter. I want to see what she knows. Maybe her grandmother killed Rachael or even one of her kids because they were angry." Mazie scribbled daughter and mother in an offshoot of Rachael's name.

She put the marker down and tapped on her phone.

"Hi, this is Emma Lee Raines from Sleepy Hollow, Kentucky." My name flowed off Mazie's tongue as if she'd been claiming my name as much as she claimed her own.

My jaw dropped. Sheepishly she looked at me and smiled. I lowered my eyes trying to figure out what she was doing and who she was talking to.

"I'm with the Sleepy Hollow PD," she spoke so fast I wasn't sure the person on the other line heard her correctly, "and I'm calling to inquire about your mother, Rachael Bemis."

I had to give a hand to Mazie. If she wanted something done, she did it.

"Mmm-hmmm. Yes. Oh, I see." Mazie nodded as if the person on the other end could see her. "It's my understanding that she's still not been found. Is that correct?"

"Ask her about her job and Kevin," I whispered as I snapped my fingers to get Mazie's attention.

"Did she ever mention the man's name?" Mazie probed. "I see that here. How about her job at Rent A Room? Did she ever talk about anyone there?"

Mazie yammered on about Rachael and I watched Granny from the window as she stood in the middle of the square looking around. She was framing different angles with her hands in the air and her eyes squinted to get a good view of whatever she was doing. There was something stuck in the back end of the waistband of her pants. But I couldn't make it out.

"She's not contacted anyone since she disappeared?" Mazie continued to hammer the poor girl with questions.

"Yes. Mmmhhh. Sleepy Hollow, Kentucky."

"No." I shook my head. "Don't tell her again."

Something inside my gut told me that Mazie needed a lesson in how to investigate in person by keeping things so vague the other person couldn't remember. On second thought, Mazie could be the computer investigator and I'd do the live things.

"Yes. Thank you. You've been so helpful." Mazie flipped her phone shut. "What?"

"Did she ask you where you were?"

"She asked." Mazie looked at me like I was crazy.

"You can't do that. If you're going to help me in this crazy job." I circled my hand in the air. "When you talk to people, you have to be so vague that they only remember you were from some police department and the reason you were there."

"She asked." Mazie must've thought it was enough of a reason.

"Then you hang up or excuse yourself. There are ways for you to get out of it. That way, they can't trace you back to the police station. I'm sure she's checking out everything you were saying and if the police find out that we used their name, they'll file charges against us."

"Us?" Mazie drew back. "I used your name."

"Thanks, Mazie." A big sigh escaped me. "What did she say? Anything new?"

"She said that they think Rachael ran off with her boyfriend. Rachael actually left town about a week before Betsy went missing." She wrote on the white board as she rambled on.

Mazie was still writing away on the dry erase board all the things Rachael's daughter had told her when Rachael and Betsy appeared.

"Hey you two. Do you think y'all can hang around and answer a few questions?" I asked them.

Mazie stared at me in a way that the other citizens of Sleepy Hollow looked at me when they thought I had the Funeral Trauma.

"You can't look at me like that if you're going to help me." I cocked a brow.

"Oh." She looked startled. "I'm sorry. It's just that I'm fascinated."

"Betsy, Rachael took you from your home and put you in the barn. Mr. Strauss had no idea you and Mr. Whiskers were in the barn when he set it on fire. He went to jail for a long time for the arson." I wanted Betsy to understand me.

"I'm so sorry." Rachael bent down to Betsy. "I didn't mean for anything to happen to you. I was being an ugly grown up. I never wanted you to die."

"What's going on?" Mazie looked between me and the space I was staring at.

"Rachael is apologizing for taking Betsy out of her home. But what doesn't make sense to me is that in the past, my other Betweener clients crossed over when they figured out how they died or who killed them. In Betsy's case, she was a victim of an arson that was never meant to kill her." I wasn't sure how this was playing out or what I needed to do to get Betsy to the other side.

"We are pretty sure Rachael was murdered. I'm thinking," Mazie made big circles around Rachael's name, "that someone killed Rachael and since Rachael was the reason Betsy was in the barn, they are tied until we figure out who killed Rachael."

"Plus Mr. Whiskers." Betsy nodded. "Why did you take me from my bed?"

"I was being a stupid grown up." She looked at Betsy. "Kevin did love you." Rachael was confessing her secrets to the little girl. "One time when we were working, he drank a little too much and had confessed that he really wanted to know what it was like to be with your mommy without children." Rachael's voice cracked, "I was a bad person and fell in love with him while we worked together. I wanted him for myself. When he picked you and your mommy, I wanted to take you to get them to break up over a fight or something silly like that."

Rachael had left out the part about them having the affair, which was probably best because I wasn't sure just how much Betsy would've understood that.

"You told me that they were going to send me off and I went with you. You lied to me. I want my mommy!" Betsy started to throw a hissy fit before she disappeared.

Mr. Whiskers hissed and disappeared shortly after.

"She took responsibility for Betsy's disappearance. She left off the fact that she and Kevin had slept together," I told Mazie.

Mazie drew a triangle. On each point she wrote Kevin, Rachael and Kay. Neither Kay nor Kevin had gotten married after all these years. Kevin wasn't in town the day of the disappearance so I'm thinking he didn't know Rachael had done it and that's how he passed the lie detector. But who knew Rachael was there and who knew she had an affair with Kevin?

"What's going on in that head of yours?" Mazie asked me.

I held up a finger.

"What on earth did you do for a week before the disappearance?" I asked Rachael.

"It's so fuzzy. I don't remember." She rubbed the pad of her finger on that same spot on her chest.

"Why do you keep rubbing your chest?" I asked.

"I don't know." Frustration hung in her words. "I don't know!"

In an instant, she was gone.

"Ask her if she remembers where she was last? Maybe that'll get us to some bones like Betsy did." Mazie shrugged, her dry erase marker at the ready.

"That's a good idea, but she's gone." I rolled my eyes. "They want to cross over, but I've learned they get so mad when questions are asked."

"Maybe she's avoiding the question like people do in life. Or she's embarrassed by the answer." Mazie made good excuses.

"That sort of behavior isn't going to help me get them over." I stood a step back and looked at the board. I pointed to Kay's name. "Kay said that there was a petting zoo and all sorts of people there for Betsy's party. I wonder if any of them saw Rachael lingering around?"

"Good." Mazie pointed the felt tip toward me before she started to underline Rachael's name. "And I'm sure she took photos of the event. We need her to bring those tonight."

"Great idea!" I was actually enjoying going back and forth with Mazie on possible ideas. Not that Jack Henry wasn't a great co-Betweener but he was so logical where Mazie had a great imagination. She put a spin on all the ideas.

The knock on the office door made Mazie and me nearly jump out of our skins. Dealing with ghosts always kept me on edge.

"Jack." It was so refreshing to see his face.

"Hi, Jack Henry." Mazie grabbed her purse. "I'm going to go make that phone call." Her purse flung behind her shoulder. "I'll talk to you tonight."

Jack Henry gave Mazie a slight nod when she walked past him and out of the office. He stared at me under hooded brows before they slid over to the big white board with all the evidence me and Mazie had written down.

"Yep." He rocked back on his heels. "I got a call from Serena Bemis."

"Oh." I looked back at the board.

"She said that you called claiming you were with the Sleepy Hollow PD and were reopening her mother's case. She never knew her mother had ties to Sleepy Hollow other than to the owner of Rent A Room. Now she's on her way here."

There wasn't an speck on his face that appeared to be happy.

"Jack." I rushed over to him and tucked my hand in the crook of his arm. "I didn't call her. Mazie did and trust me, I wasn't happy that she used my name."

"Why does Mazie have any involvement in this?" He looked at me.

"She knows I'm a Betweener." I gulped.

"Emma Lee, this is exactly what we feared." He reminded me of how much we've tried to keep my little secret under wraps and the idea of what would happen if anyone found out.

"You're the one who's leaving me here to do this alone." I gulped and immediately wished I could take back my words. "I mean…"

He jerked his arm away from me.

"I understand that me taking a job is putting a strain on our relationship, but you pretending to be a cop is an offense punishable by law. What would've happened if someone else at the office took the call? They'd investigate by taking phone records and put you and Mazie in jail." He was always so by the book. "As far as your Betweener clients, I know that me leaving puts you alone. They aren't here to see me. You were doing just fine before you told me about your gift."

My eyes welled with tears. As much as I tried to put on my big girl pants and sniff them back, there were just too many and like a dam breaking, they flooded right on out and down my face.

"Mazie knew just like you that I had a gift. She said she'd been watching my actions closely and saw how tied you and I were to the cases. She's also got great internet skills that I lack, so I figured I'd tell her the truth." I sucked back more tears. "I don't think I can do it on my own and Mazie has some great ideas."

I pointed to the board.

Jack didn't bother looking at it. He pulled me to his chest. He used the pad of his finger to tip my chin up to look at him. His soft lips covered mine. He held me tighter.

"I'm not upset that you and Mazie are playing Nancy Drew." He smiled. "But you can't go around pretending to be the police. I told Serena that we hadn't reopened any case but we are looking into a case related to her mother's boss. She's still coming here. Now I have to get the Chicago police involved. But I'd like to be able to give them something. Like bones. Can you ask Rachael where she was when she was murdered?"

"Don't you think I've done that?" I pointed to the board where Mazie had stuck Rachael's photo next to her name. "Her chest," I gasped and hurried over to the photo. "What is around her neck?"

"Now you've lost me." Jack Henry came over and looked at the picture Mazie had found on the internet.

"Rachael continues to rub her chest when we are talking. I thought it was some sort of nervous habit, but now I think she's looking for something." I put my finger on her photo. "And I think that something is right there."

Both of us leaned in. She was wearing a necklace, but the object was out of focus.

"I'll check into it. But I'm not sure how that can help us," he said.

This was where I was saying Mazie and I made a better team. She'd be throwing ideas out while Jack Henry had to see the physical and practical evidence.

"Okay." It was easier to agree with him at this point. "Tomorrow night we are having a vigil for the anniversary of Betsy's disappearance and now death. Mazie was going to get the media here to cover it as well as those big balloons to let go. She had a good idea that she's seen on TV where the killer usually shows up at events like these, but now that I know the killer—"

"You know the killer?" Jack Henry's jaw tensed. "You know who killed Betsy?"

"Rachael Bemis." I just realized I'd yet to tell him of the discovery.

"Emma. What are you talking about." He braced himself up against Charlotte's desk.

I proceeded to tell him how Rachael was in love with Kevin and how she took Betsy.

"So technically, she didn't kill Betsy. But someone did kill her and that's why I think they are my Betweener clients. I think Betsy and Rachael are so connected in the afterlife, they've both got to have the killer brought to justice," I said.

"And here I thought you had two separate Betweener cases going." He eased himself up off the desk. "I'm not going to call Chicago until you find me evidence that she's involved. Don't go around telling anyone that you are with the force either. I've got to cover your tracks."

"I'm sorry. I did tell Mazie after the fact that she couldn't do that." There was a tug on my heart.

The thought that he was going to be leaving me for a few months had started to settle in the deep parts of my heart.

"Can we forget about all of this the rest of the night and just enjoy each other?" he asked and walked back over to me, taking me into his arms once again.

Chapter Nineteen

"Happy birthday to you! Happy birthday day to you!" Granny yelped at five a.m.

"Happy birfday to you!" Betsy chimed in.

"Happy birthday, dear Emma Lee! Happy birthday to you!" Granny continued to belt out the tune until I rolled over.

The thirty lit candles on top of the cake weren't nearly as bright as Granny's smile.

"Get up! You know, I'll never forget your daddy waking me up that morning." She told the same story about my birth the same time, every single year. Five a.m. "Yep. It was about midnight. We'd just buried three people that day and we were so tired. I swear you came because your mama had spent so much time on her feet that day. Three funerals was a lot."

I threw back the covers. I refrained from reciting the story by heart. Even though I was there and didn't remember, I really could tell it like I did remember it.

"I swear that doctor had to pluck you out because you weren't coming." She cackled and set the burning cake on the bedside table.

"Go on, get up. It's about five o'clock and you've got to blow out them candles and make a wish." Granny had the superstition that if you made a wish at the exact time of your birth, they'd come true.

I even subscribed to her crazy notion that this was true after Jack Henry and I started dating. Then the wishes turned into marriage. Here we were today. No ring. No marriage. And soon no Jack Henry.

"Thanks, Granny." I knew she had such good intentions.

"Well, if I were you, and clearly I'm not because I have no problems getting married." She threw her head back and laughed again. "I'd not waste a wish on Jack Henry."

"How did you know I wish for Jack Henry?" I asked.

"You're old granny ain't so stupid or crazy." She winked. "Go on. Blow them candles out before you catch the funeral home on fire."

Granny and I spent a couple of hours before the sun came up to reminisce about old times and even had a good time visiting about Charlotte.

The next few hours I returned some phone calls for Eternal Slumber and took a few birthday calls. Jack Henry sent me a bouquet of daisies with a request to join him for supper. And to dress nice.

By the time I finished up some business, it was almost time to meet Mazie before the big vigil. She'd texted to let me know that she'd called Kay. I'd texted back to have her meet me at Higher Grounds.

The late day sun was setting over the courthouse. The tall steeple on the oldest building in Sleepy Hollow looked so majestic in the golden sunset. In a much different life than the one I had now, I used to lie in the grass in the square and watch the sunset dreaming of seeing this same sunset with Jack Henry for the rest of my life. Our relationship, though not as I had pictured it six months ago, will be able to withstand anything that was going to be thrown at us and that included the state police stint. Tonight, after the vigil, I was ready to kick off my shoes, relax and enjoy a nice quiet evening with the only man I've ever loved.

"There's the birthday girl!" Cheryl Lynne yelled when I walked through the door. "I've been waiting for you." She reached behind the counter and stuck a cupcake on top of it. There was a fondant E on the top. "I've been waiting for you all day. Your favorite."

"Red velvet?" I let out a big squeal. "You are a good friend." I reached up and grabbed it.

"Hey. What about me?" Mazie asked from behind. She still had her light blue library polo and khaki pants on with her white tennis shoes. "Happy birthday." She had a cute orange gift bag dangling from her finger. "For you. I got it from Southern Roots. I figured you could use it for Zula's wedding."

"Thanks." I took the package. "Can we get a couple of coffees?" I turned back to Cheryl.

"I'll pay for them." Mazie chimed in with a happy nod and a smile on her face.

I looked between the two of them as they started to chat about what was going on in their lives and I felt a little better about Jack Henry leaving. I'd never really realized that I did have a couple of good friends here. I knew they'd be here for me.

"Are you ready?" Mazie grabbed both coffees and we headed toward the open café table in the front of the coffee shop. "I called Kay and she said that she didn't know where the photos of that party were. But she'd let us know when she found them."

"It wasn't like we gave her much notice. Jack Henry and I were talking last night. My biggest fear came true." I peeled the cupcake paper off the delicious birthday treat. My mouth watered at the sight of the moist red cake. "Serena Bemis called Jack Henry and asked him about the open investigation because she checked with the Chicago PD and they didn't know anything about it. And you used my name, which she wrote down."

"I'm so sorry. I promise I'll do better next time." There was sincerity in the tone of her voice. "Did she give him any clues to her mom?"

"No," my voice muffled from the big bite I'd stuffed into my mouth. "She's coming to town to talk to him or something. I don't know. All I know is that we've got to figure out where Rachael is in order for Jack to really open the case."

"Hopefully the killer will show up tonight and we can get them." Mazie had no idea how this thing played out.

It wasn't as easy as she'd thought and I felt like we were at a dead end.

"I asked Fluggie Callahan to come do a story for the paper and local news crews. I hope it gets some coverage and is picked up nationally. Even though we know what happened to Betsy, the world doesn't know yet. Or did Jack Henry tell Kay?" she asked before taking a sip of her coffee.

"He won't say anything until we can prove Rachael was connected to Betsy and how she got her." That was going to be hard to do with Rachael being dead. We'd have to have hard evidence to prove it.

"Tonight. Tonight is going to be it." She gave a firm nod and looked out the window. "The news is here."

There was a white news van pulled up on the inn side of the square. Fluggie Callahan was sitting on the gazebo steps. She never missed a good scoop.

"Fluggie is already there," I noted.

"Yeah. We sorta made a deal. She loves to read romance novels and I've got my pulse on all the new releases." Mazie was sneaky and I loved it.

"Do tell." My jaw dropped. I never imagined Fluggie ever reading romance.

"Oh yeah. Her favorite author, who writes smut, has a new book coming out next week and I told her I'd hold it for her if, and only if, she took photos of the event and let me have a disc of them. Because I'm telling you, the killer will come back." She wiggled her brows with a smirk on her face.

"You are awesome." I laughed at her bribing skills. "And I like it. I hope you're right about the killer." I leaned over. "It'd have to be Rachael's killer because we know Betsy was accidentally killed by the barn fire."

"Someone in this entire crazy situation knows." She eased back in the café chair.

"Rachael always does this." I took my finger and rubbed the middle of my chest like Rachael did. "I wasn't sure why she does it, but when Jack Henry came by the funeral home and looked at the white board, I noticed in the photo you found of Rachael on the internet, she has on a necklace. I can't tell what it is. I wonder if she had it on when she died. If she did, her bones might be deteriorated, but not the necklace."

"We can ask her daughter tonight if she shows up at the vigil. Or did Jack Henry not tell her about it?" Mazie asked.

"I'm not sure why he'd invite her to that especially since he hadn't yet known what you and I have found out." I took a drink of the coffee and noticed out of the corner of my eye there was a group of people who were already gathered at the square. There was also a table set up with some big white paper balloons that I was sure were the ones we were going to light and send up into the sky.

"Emma Lee," Rachael appeared next to Mazie. Her eyes were hollow and scared.

"Birthday girl," Cheryl called after me. My eyes slid from Rachael to Cheryl. "This lady is looking for Jack Henry."

"That lady is my daughter," Rachael whispered. Her finger rubbing her chest as if she were rubbing out the hurt.

Chapter Twenty

I pretended to text Jack Henry and took Serena by the arm, leading her over to the café table where I pulled a chair up for her to sit. Not that I wasn't going to really text Jack, I was, but in due time.

"Mazie, this is Serena Bemis." I hoped Mazie wouldn't be freaked out. Trial by fire, right? "She's the one I called about her mom Rachael."

At this point, Rachael wasn't leaving Serena's side. She continued to beg for Serena's forgiveness. I wasn't able to tell Serena that because it was very apparent Serena felt like her mother was still alive and living some life with the man she'd run off with.

"When I called you back, Sheriff Ross answered and he didn't seem to know about reopening the investigation. That's why I decided to come here. I don't understand why Sleepy Hollow PD would reopen her case when the Chicago PD continued to say that she ran off since there weren't any signs of her." Serena was confused. "She gave me and my brother to our grandmother and took off."

"Does your grandmother remember anything that your mom said about coming back?" I asked. "For the investigation."

"Shouldn't you take me to the station for a statement or something? Or at least write it down?" She looked around the café.

"We do our best work right here. Besides, we have a vigil for a little girl that disappeared twenty years ago today. She was a cold case too." Mazie made it sound so good. "Since both of us are here, we have good memories."

"They sure do things differently in Kentucky." Serena scooted up on the edge of the chair. "My grandmother claims that she thought my mom was always coming back. She also said she didn't know who the man was. We had our suspicions since he'd given her a gift and she never took it off."

"Did it happen to be a necklace?" I asked.

"Yes." Rachael and Serena said in unison. "He gave me a little TV charm and I put it on a necklace chain."

"She put it on a chain," Serena followed up. "I really think it was someone she worked with because they sold and rented furniture, including TVs. She didn't get it until she took the job and she didn't ever take it off."

"Where did it go?" Rachael rubbed her finger to her chest. "I never took it off."

"Jack Henry," I jumped in my surprise to see him walking down the sidewalk toward the café. "I'll be right back."

I left Serena with Mazie. Something I probably shouldn't have done because I wasn't sure how Mazie would act and if she'd pretend to be someone and say something that'd get us in trouble, but I did anyway. Having Jack Henry mad at me was by far worse in my humble opinion.

"Hi." I bounced on my toes. He looked so handsome in his brown uniform. "Thank you for the flowers. I'm so excited about tonight."

"Happy birthday, baby." He tucked a strand of hair behind my ear and rested the palm of his hand on the back of my neck, pulling me to him for a gentle kiss.

"And it just gets better." Out of the corner of my eye, I could see the door of Higher Grounds open and Serena coming out. "But I have to tell you that Serena. . ."

'Hi, Sheriff, I'm Serena Bemis." She stuck her hand out. "Officer Raines and I were just discussing the necklace my mother always wore."

"Necklace, huh?" His loving hand dropped from me and distrusting eyes stared at me. "Why don't you and I go on down to the station to get your statement?"

"They," she pointed to Mazie, and me "said they usually did their interviews here."

"They did, did they?" His brows rose. "I'll take you on down to the station while they work the vigil." He nodded at me.

"Yes, sir. Sir." Mazie clicked her heels together like she was in the army and did the salute too.

"Stop it," I whispered and grabbed her hand, flinging it down to her side. "We'll do that and I'll see you afterward."

Jack didn't even tell me bye. The stalk in his walk told me he was very unhappy with keeping Serena at Higher Grounds. Mazie and I watched as Serena got into Jack's cruiser and they took off.

"That was close." Mazie swiped her hand across her brow. "Shhhew."

"I'll hear about it later." There was a sick feeling in my gut. "Isn't that Kay?"

The media and Fluggie had already surrounded her. Mazie and I scurried across the street.

"You keep her company and I'll watch Rachael's reaction to the people." I looked around for Rachael and realized she was probably with her daughter, but Betsy and Mr. Whiskers were in the gazebo going around and around in circles, having a great time.

I didn't tell Mazie that because I needed to really look around and Mazie needed a job. Her job was to make sure the vigil went smoothly.

Betsy spent most of her time looking at her mom and Mr. Whiskers spent the night napping in the gazebo.

"What's he doing here?" Mazie walked up and pointed out that Kevin Allen had shown up. He and Kay were talking. There weren't any smiles or warm fuzzies coming from either of them.

"I'm not sure." I watched Betsy. She reached out and touched Kevin. He brought that hand up to his chest before trying to reach out to Kay. Kay jerked away. "He felt Betsy touch him."

"Is Betsy mad?"

"No." I shook my head.

"You'd think she'd be mad at him." Mazie shrugged.

"Why? Because he cheated on her mother? I'm not even sure if Kay knew about that since Kay said she didn't recognize the name when we asked her about it." I continued to watch the uncomfortable exchange between the two.

"Seeing them together like this just makes me think Kay knows that Kevin did something. Whether it was with Rachael or to Betsy, but something is wrong." Mazie had a good instinct because I was feeling it too.

"Here she comes." I straightened up when I saw Kay coming toward us.

"I'm ready to get this over with." She looked around. "Do you think Betsy's killer is here?" There was sadness in her voice.

"We'll see." I offered a smile and kept my head down so Kevin didn't see me.

Mazie took over and gave a little speech with Kay next to her. Even Pastor Brown was there to offer a blessing and

a prayer. Fluggie's camera clicked and flashed. There were
so many people there I didn't know, that I hoped one of
them would give Betsy some sort of memory. Or even a
memory for Rachael. Everyone had one of the paper
balloons and together lit the bottom causing them to all
float up in the air. I turned and looked around at Betsy and
Mr. Whiskers in the gazebo. It was good to see Rachael had
joined them. The three of them stood on the top step in the
exact same place I'd seen them for the first time six months
ago. My heart sank. I was no closer to helping them cross
over tonight as I was then.

"What on earth are those?" Granny came up and
brought me out of my own head where I was beating
myself up. "I want them at my nuptials. And we never went
to that bridal shop."

"I need to go because Mazie got me something from
there and I want to check the place out. We can go
tomorrow afternoon." I put my arm around her. "Do you
think Charlotte can see all of this from up above?"

"She has her loving hand all over us, Emma Lee."
Granny squeezed my waist where her arm was hooked.

Loving hand was going a little far and if Charlotte was
alive, I'd have started laughing at the statement. I did love
Charlotte, but loving was not a word I'd use to describe
her.

Granny and I stood in the dusk of the night and
watched as the balloons headed off into the still of the fall
night and disappeared behind the mountains.

Chapter Twenty-One

A small red and green sign that read Bella Vino Restorante flickered through the blinds of the window along with the tapered candle in the middle of the cream linen covered table. Jack Henry's arm extended with his hands on mine. Two glasses of wine and a chilled bottle sat on the table. If that wasn't enough to put you in a romantic mood, the authentic Italian music quietly played above from the speakers. The low lighting glowed along the pale yellow exposed brick. The entire feel of the restaurant was as if you stepped into Italy.

"I'm lucky they had a table left." He gazed at me.

"I was so excited when I got your note and flowers." I used my free hand to take lots of sips from my wine glass. It was helping keep the tears at bay.

There were only six tables in the entire restaurant, which made it very difficult to get reservations.

The waitress came out with large steaming family style bowls. One was filled with spaghetti noodles, another filled with large hand rolled meatballs, and the other with sauce. The bread basket was overflowing with breadsticks with a heavy garlic smell.

Jack Henry took my plate and filled it for me, being the good southern gentleman that he was. He held the bread basket over the table for me to take one.

"I told my mom about the job today." Jack Henry tore his breadstick in half and dipped it into the sauce on his plate. "Her reaction actually surprised me."

"Really?" Hearing what his mother had to say was something I could probably do without. She wasn't a fan of the last time he'd turned down the offer because of me. I rarely went to her house to visit and when I did, she made me feel like my job was menial. Plus, she was a Burns person. That really ticked me off.

"Yeah. She said that she didn't understand why now and what about me and you." He smiled. "I think she's coming around to the idea of us."

"About time," I muttered.

"She said that she didn't know if she liked the fact I wasn't going to be living here anymore and not seeing me was going to be bad for her." His eyes lowered. He gave a wry smile. "If I didn't know better, I'd think you two were in cahoots."

"Trust me, we're not." I assured him and downed the last sip of wine. "What did Serena have to say?"

It was time to change the subject. If he kept talking about his new job and leaving me, I would drink the entire bottle and that wasn't a pretty sight. My crying face was ugly, but my drunk crying face was worse.

"Same stuff that was reported when she was a kid. She's not heard from her mom and she had no idea who the man was," he said.

"I do know that the necklace in the photo is a TV charm. Apparently Kevin gave it to her, but I've not seen her since the vigil to ask. Mazie had Fluggie taking all sorts of photos because she said that all the books she read and researched, the killer loves to show up at things like that." I grabbed another breadstick to help soak up the wine that was now making me light-headed. "Rachael doesn't have a necklace on. She keeps rubbing that area and I know if we find the necklace, we'll find her bones."

"That's all great, but we have no leads. I had to let Serena go home with the notion we couldn't open the case." Jack Henry didn't make me feel any better about the case.

"I can't let these two just linger around and not let them have some sort of peace." Screw the bread. I grabbed the bottle and filled my glass up with the remaining wine. "That's awful. A Betweener not able to help her clients. What a joke," I whispered into the glass and took a big gulp.

That bothered me more than Jack Henry leaving. With him leaving, I'd still have Betweener clients to keep me busy, maybe. But if word got around up in the beyond that I wasn't able to help them, they'd stop coming to see me. I was starting to really like that job. I felt like I was making a difference and bringing justice to the world one murderer at a time.

"Enough about that. It'll work its way out." His face hardened. "I'm leaving next week."

"Next week?" My eyes popped open. "Why so soon?"

"The sooner I'm gone, the quicker I'll be back." His face was so serious, it scared me. "If I don't like it, I've figured it out. But you were right a few months back."

"What did I say?" I couldn't even remember.

"You told me that if I didn't try it, I'd always wonder and maybe become bitter and mad at myself."

That sounded like something I'd say, but I didn't mean a word of it. I'd like to kick my own butt right now. I mean wallop myself good. A scowl formed across my face.

"Did I?" I asked and forced a smile. "We'll be fine. And if you do like it, we can figure that out too."

"I can be stationed locally probably, I'd just have to drive to work." By driving to work, he meant that he'd have to drive to the interstate, which wasn't close to Sleepy Hollow.

"It'd only be a fifty-minute drive." I tried to make it sound better than driving the curvy roads and driving through Lexington to get there.

"See. We've got it all worked out." There was a satisfied look on Jack Henry's face that I was going to take a mental picture of because I could tell it wasn't going to be that easy.

Chapter Twenty-Two

"Nothing?" Mazie's nose curled, her head slowly rolled back on her neck as she pushed the million photos across Charlotte Rae's desk.

"Not a single person." Rachael and Betsy had looked at the photos carefully for the past couple of hours. My eyes were beginning to blur and I needed a break.

I couldn't rule out that my eye blur wasn't due to a wine hangover from last night's date night with Jack Henry and possibly the last date in a few weeks. He'd given me promises of coming home when he was off work or not in classes with the state police, but I wasn't holding my breath. Jack Henry was an all-in kind of guy. That was one thing I loved about him. He did a job and he did it to the best of his ability. His love was no different.

Before he dropped me back off at the funeral home, I'd assured him that I was going to be right there. After all, what man wanted to date the creepy funeral home girl. The name I was affectionately called by the high school bullies, to which Jack Henry pointed out that we weren't in high school anymore and the woman I turned into was the best thing that'd come out of Sleepy Hollow.

Needless to say, his sweet words and sexy smile gave him a pass to go follow his dreams.

"I'm sorry to say that I'm at a dead end." I looked between Rachael and Betsy. Mr. Whiskers meowed and went to curl up by the vent where the heat was pumping out.

It'd turned unseasonably cold overnight. Pretty much matched how I felt in my heart.

"I've never had this happen with a Betweener client." I tried and tried to make excuses, but there were just none to make.

They ghosted away.

"What did they say?" Mazie asked.

"They left." I gathered up all the photos in a pile and took one last look at the dry erase board before I took the eraser and cleaned it off. "I'm sure they're going to tell their other friends that I'm not a good Betweener."

"Huh?" Mazie snarled.

"Remember how Ruthie Sue Payne was the biggest gossip in Sleepy Hollow before she was murdered?" I reminisced about the good ole Betweener days. Mazie nodded. "Apparently, she's just as big of a gossip in the afterlife. That's how murdered ghosts found out about me. Not Betsy. She said Charlotte told her."

Then it hit me. If Charlotte Rae believed in me enough to send clients, there had to be something I was missing.

"I'm going to go tell Kay what we found out about Rachael." Jack Henry hadn't given me permission to tell anyone anything about that part of the case, but I felt at least Kay should have some sort of closure and maybe that was enough to get Betsy and Mr. Whiskers to cross over.

At least I hoped so.

Mazie had to work the rest of the day at the Sleepy Hollow Library and I'd taken a call to pick up a body from the hospital. Natural death of old age. At least I'd be spending the next week doing a funeral instead of wallowing in self-pity from Jack leaving.

When I pulled up in front of Kay's house, my stomach dropped. Betsy and Mr. Whiskers had gone with me. Both of them sat in the front, but Rachael was nowhere to be found. Maybe my plan was right. I'd tell Kay about Rachael and then I'd leave in hopes of seeing Betsy cross over.

"Emma Lee," Kay stood at the door. She looked a little more rested and she'd fixed her hair. "I wasn't expecting you. Do you have some news about the killer showing up?"

"Actually, I do." I gestured to the door. "May I come in?"

"Yes. I'm so sorry." She shook her head and smiled. "I guess I was so stunned to see you here."

She moved back and let me step in.

"What's going on?" I asked when I saw the stacks of brown boxes.

"Last night was an eye opener for me." She used the big roll of packing tape to strap across the box edges and used a pair of scissors to cut it. She ran a flat palm down the seam of the tape. "I think it was actually closure for me. I'm not sure who would've put Betsy in the barn, but there is some comfort in knowing after all these years she not still searching for me. I can move and even though I'm an old lady, I'm still breathing and can make something out of the rest of my life." She looked around, shaking her head. "I've stayed here all these years waiting for her to show up on my doorstep."

A tear fell down her cheek. I looked around for a Kleenex.

"I'd give you a tissue if I could find one." The edges of my eyes dipped seeing her sad and Betsy trying to reassure her mother. "I do have a theory about Betsy's death that might come as a shock to you and it actually opens up another cold case. I think they are related."

"Really?" There was a gasp of relief from her.

"I think you might be a little shocked and a nice move away will probably be the best thing for you." I watched as she brushed away her tears. "Remember when I asked you about Rachael Bemis?"

She nodded. The tears continued to flow down her face. Now I was feeling bad for stopping by.

"Well, I've gotten some information that she and Kevin had slept together while he was engaged to you." I stopped when her face jerked up. Her mouth dropped opened. "She was from the Chicago office. She wanted to break the two of you up, so she snuck in and took Betsy to that barn. She was going to let her go, but that's when Mr. Strauss set it on fire. He'd not even checked to see if anyone was in the barn or he would've saved her. This explains why she was bound and gagged."

"How do you know this?" The tears became sobs. "I've got to get a tissue." She scurried out of the room.

I reached out and opened the box that was next to be taped up. It wouldn't hurt to help her.

When I looked inside, there were some photos of Betsy. She looked so happy with her mom. There was one with a bouncy house. Another with some lizards. In the background, I could see it was from the mansion. Then it dawned on me. It had to be from the last party she'd thrown for Betsy.

I couldn't wait to tell Mazie that she found them. It was a great memory for Kay because Betsy was smiling in all of them.

"She knew I was there." Rachael appeared. "I remember. I went to the party and I pretended to be with the bouncy house employees. She recognized me."

"How did she recognize you?" I asked and took out several photos at one time.

"There." Rachael pointed to the photo. "There I am."

The bouncy house was the focus of the photo. Off to the side, Kay looked to be confronting Rachael.

"She told me to come back and we'd discuss it that night. That's when I took Betsy and later in the early morning, I showed up to talk to her. I was planning on telling her to leave Kevin and I'd tell her where Betsy was." She rubbed her chest with her finger.

"What happened when you came back?" I asked and when I saw something shiny in the box, I reached down and grabbed the necklace with the TV charm dangling off of it.

"Excuse me?" Kay came back into the room.

"Mommy didn't mean to." Betsy looked between Rachael and me. "Mommy loves me," she cried out.

"Umm. Nothing." I planted a smile on my face and decided to leave. I had to call Jack Henry. I dropped the photo and the necklace in the box. Kay's eyes followed the photo and she looked up at me, eyes dry as a bone. "Again, I'm just speculating that all that happened with Rachael Bemis because she's still on the run."

"No. She's dead. And you know it." Kay reached for the scissors.

I lunged toward them, but she was too quick.

"Why don't you have a seat and we'll talk." By the way she was pointing to the kitchen with the scissors, I didn't think there was room for negotiation. "I'm not saying that Kevin was right. We did need some time together. I wasn't opposed to sending Betsy off to boarding school, but I certainly wasn't going to play house here while he played sex games with little Miss Hussy in Chicago. Before Kevin left for that trip, he promised me he was going to break if off with her and when she showed up, I decided I'd do it for them. I had no idea that bitch stole my kid."

The Mama Kay persona wasn't as appealing as it had been at first. The entire time Betsy begged her mom to stop talking. It was as if she'd known her mom's secret this whole time. She stood in front of me in the kitchen with the scissors pointed at me. A good shanking wasn't how I planned on joining Charlotte Rae.

"We can go to Jack and he'd see this as a crime of passion. He'd totally understand. Besides," I pish-poshed her hoping she'd fall for it, "the statue of limitations has passed. I don't blame you. I'd have done the same thing."

I lied.

A sigh of relief escaped me when I saw Jack Henry appear over her shoulder in her hallway. She looked behind her to see what I was looking at.

"Hold it right there, Kay." Jack Henry stared down the sight of his gun. "Kevin and his housekeeper Lu came in to see me today. They told me everything."

"They can't prove nothing," she spat back at him.

"The evidence is in the box along with Rachael Bemis's necklace Kevin gave her." I couldn't help myself.

Betsy and Rachael watched as the other officers had come in and taken Kay off in handcuffs.

"How did you know I was here?" I asked Jack Henry.

"I didn't." He wasn't happy. "I came here to arrest her after Kevin Allen and his housekeeper came to tell me. In fact, Kevin had no idea what happened to Rachael. Last night after he told Lu about the vigil, she broke down and told him that she saw Rachael there and Kay told her to leave. Then she saw Kay digging in the garden. Me and a couple of my men went out there and found Rachael's bones."

"Wow." I was in bit of a shock. "I never imagined it'd go down this way."

Betsy and Rachael were in the corner hugging each other. Rachael looked as if she were comforting Betsy.

"Let's get you out of here." Jack Henry held his hand out for me to take.

"Can I stay for one second?" I held a finger up. Without having to explain I needed time with my clients, he knew.

"Yeah." He smiled. "But you're going to have to give up this job when I leave for the state police because I have no idea who's going to save you from all of this."

I laughed.

When the coast was clear, I went into the family room looking for Betsy and Rachael. Both of them were standing over the box where I'd found the photos. Mr. Whiskers was rubbing himself on my ankles. I guessed it was his way of thanking me.

"I guess this is goodbye." Rachael dropped Betsy's hand. She looked over her right shoulder. A bright white light appeared as a dot and quickly got bigger. "That's my ride to the other side. Thank you, Emma Lee." She bent down to Betsy. "I'm so sorry. All of this is because of me. If I could go back twenty years, I'd do it all differently."

She and Betsy hugged before she disappeared into the light.

"How about that book you promised me?" Betsy's little voice broke the silence that was left after Rachael had crossed over.

"I'd love to." I reached in the box and pulled out one of Betsy's books. I sat on the couch and opened it. She snuggled up next to me.

Before I could even get the first word out, a big rainbow appeared.

Betsy gasped as I did too. Mr. Whiskers jumped up and hopped on. When he got halfway across the rainbow bridge, he turned around and gave a little meow before he darted over the bridge.

Chapter Twenty-Three

"How have you been?" Granny pulled one of the
wedding dresses that suited her age off the rack of Southern
Roots and held it up to her body looking into the full-length
mirror.

"I heard from Jack Henry." I shrugged. My head tilted
to the side to get a look at her. I gave her the thumbs down.
She stuck it back on the rack and we started pushing and
tugging on more. "He's working long hours. He'd had a
couple of ride-alongs already. He said it's a lot of speeding
tickets."

"He'll not like it. Mark my words." Granny nodded
and pulled out another dress. She held it up toward Mazie
to look at.

Mazie shook her head.

I'd been lucky that Mazie and I'd become friends.
She'd been a lifesaver over the past couple of months while
Jack was gone. We'd been to movies, cooked at the Inn,
even taken a yoga class or two from Hettie Bell. It was time
for me to make good on my promise to Granny to help pick
out a dress for her crazy wedding to poor old Doc Clyde. I
still didn't think he knew what he was getting himself into.

It'd been hard without Jack Henry, but not impossible.
The fear of being alone the rest of my life had started to
creep in. I wasn't alone. Though I could tell by Jack
Henry's voice that he was having a great time. He liked
learning about the drug trafficking on the interstates and he
also got to have a drug dog with him on some of the ride-
alongs. He talked on and on about it.

"What about this one?" Granny snarled in the mirror.

"Nah." I took a couple of steps back and turned around.

Southern Roots was an adorable clothing store. One side was just a boutique of clothes that a girl of thirty could fit into. The walls of the boutique were reclaimed wood and looked as if we were inside a barn. The floors were dark stained hardwood. There were chandeliers hanging from the ceiling with pearls and crystals draped all over them and hanging down.

The cutest sweater hung from one of the displays in the front window that I'd noticed when Granny and I had come in. While Granny looked around, I decided to mosey up there and take a gander.

Immediately, I saw a man standing next to my hearse. He was in a brown sheriff's uniform and looking at my license plate. I ran out of the shop.

"Hey. What are you doing?" I demanded an answer.

"Is this your. . .um. . ." He looked down the hearse.

"My hearse?" I asked and snarled. "Yes. Are you writing me a ticket?"

"Are you picking up a dead body?" he asked back with a little sarcasm.

I tugged the edges of my jacket up around my neck. I wasn't sure if it was the cold weather or this man's cold demeanor he was giving off.

"No." My brows furrowed.

"Then yep. You're getting a ticket." He smiled. His dimples deepened and I noticed his bright green eyes under his curly blond hair. "You're parked illegally. As the interim sheriff, I'm going to whip this town into shape."

I stood there unable to say anything. Jack Henry had been replaced.

"Good day." He nodded and I swear he winked after I took the ticket.

"Who was that hunk?" Mazie came out of the shop. Both of us stared as the new man in town got into the Sleepy Hollow sheriff's cruiser and drove off.

Read on for a sneak peek at

Tonya Kappes's

newest cozy mystery series

Killer Coffee Mystery Series!

Starting with

SCENE

OF THE GRIND

NOW AVAILABLE!

Chapter One

Drip, drip, drip.

There is something about coffee that brings people together. And they don't even have to like coffee. Is it the smell? Is it the comforting sound of the drip? I don't know. All I did know was that my new coffee shop in the touristy lake town of Honey Springs, Kentucky, The Bean Hive, was opened for business.

"Seven a.m.," I muttered after I'd glanced up at the clock and drew my eyes back out the front doors of the coffeehouse located in the best spot on the boardwalk that ran along Lake Honey Springs.

The boardwalk held fond memories for me since I used to spend my summers here with my Aunt Maxine. Maxi for short. For the past year my life was stalled in a little bit of what I'd call a fork in the road, so after hearing Aunt Maxi talk about all the revitalization of the boardwalk and not really knowing what to do, it sounded like a splendid idea to open a shop. At the time.

The annual Honey Festival was in a couple of days and all the vendors and the new shops on the boardwalk were holding a grand opening. I'd already had the coffeehouse ready to open since when I moved to Honey Springs a few weeks ago, I made it a point to no longer sit around resting on my laurels, so I opened the shop a few days early. Which might not've been the best business plan since my only customers had been a few stragglers here and there.

Mainly construction workers who were working day and night to get the shops ready for the big festival.

The Bean Hive was located in the middle of the boardwalk, right across from the pier. It was a perfect spot and I was beyond thrilled with the exposed brick walls and wooden ceiling beams that I didn't have to touch. Luckily, Aunt Maxi owned the place. The rent was a little steep, but I'd watched a few DIY videos on YouTube to figure out how to make the necessary repairs for inspection. I couldn't be more pleased with the shiplap wall I'd created myself out of plywood painted white to make it look like real shiplap.

Instead of investing in a fancy menu or even menu boards that attached to the wall, I'd bought four large chalkboards that hung down from the ceiling over the L-shaped glass countertop.

The first chalkboard menu hung over the pie counter and listed the pies and cookies with their prices. The second menu hung over the tortes and quiches. The third menu before the L-shaped counter curved listed the breakfast casseroles and drinks. Over top the other counter the chalkboard listed lunch options, including soups, and catering information.

On each side of the counter was a drink stand. One was a coffee bar with six industrial thermoses with different blends of my specialty coffees as well as one filled with a decaffeinated blend, even though I clearly never understood the concept of that. But Aunt Maxi made sure I understood some people only drink the unleaded stuff. The coffee bar had everything you needed to take a coffee with you. Even an honor system where you could pay and go.

The drink bar on the opposite end of the counter was a tea bar. Hot tea, cold tea. There was a nice selection of gourmet teas and loose leaf teas along with cold teas. I'd even gotten a few antique tea pots from Wild and Whimsy Antique shop, which happened to be the first shop on the boardwalk. If a customer came in and wanted a pot of hot tea, I could fix it for them or they could fix their own to their taste.

A few café tables dotted the inside along with two long window tables with stools butted up to them on each side of the front door. It was a perfect spot to sit, enjoy the beautiful Lake Honey Springs and sip on your favorite beverage.

Which just so happened to be where I was sitting this morning enjoying the view until I realized I'd been here since four a.m. to get the casseroles made and coffees brewed before the opening time of seven a.m. and no one was here.

"You did open a little early," I said to make myself feel better and hooked my finger in the mug of freshly brewed coffee.

Curling both hands around the mug, I leaned my hip up against the counter and took a sip. Even if no one showed up today, it was better than where I was a year ago. My chin lifted as the first rays of sunshine popped through the large front windows. I closed my eyes and let the breaking of the dawn fill my soul.

It was spring in Kentucky and the leaves were starting to get their deep green color back, filling in the tree line along the lake. A few fishing boats had trolled by since it was a no wake zone. Good fishing started around five a.m. around here and they were usually back by seven. At the far end of the pier was a marina with boat slips and a really neat little restaurant, The Watershed. It was probably the fanciest restaurant in Honey Springs.

With my mug in my hands, I decided to get a whiff of the fresh air.

The bell dinged over the front door when I opened it. Cool air swept in reminding me that spring in Kentucky was cold in the morning and hot in the afternoon. Dressing was always a problem, but with the few uniform pieces I'd picked to go with my black pants and sensible shoes I'd handle the change easily. Besides, the black apron with The Bean Hive logo was amazing and I'd gotten several of those.

Today I'd decided on the thin long-sleeved crew neck and had tied the apron over it.

Since there wasn't anyone in the coffeehouse, I'd decided to stroll to the right of the coffeehouse on the boardwalk and do a little window shopping, even though most of them weren't opening until the grand opening this weekend. I walked all the way to the end and looked as I made my way back, enjoying my cup of coffee and the morning sunrise as it dripped in many colors in the lake. It was funny how water could turn the orange and yellow rays different colors as it mirrored in the lake.

The shops were really coming along. All the shops were butted next to each other with a different awning to boast the name of the shop. Every few feet there were a couple of café tables where visitors could shop and stop to enjoy each other or just the view the boardwalk gave.

Wild and Whimsy was the first shop on the boardwalk. It was an eclectic shop of antiques and repurposed furniture. Beverly and Dan Teagarden were the owners. Their two grown children, Savannah and Melanie helped them run it. Instead of the regular shingled roof, Dan had paid extra to put on a rusty tin roof to go with the store's theme. They'd kept the awning a red color but without the name. The Wild and Whimsy sign dangled down from the awning.

Honey Comb Salon & Spa was located next and it was a fancy, for Honey Springs, salon. Alice Dee Spicer was the owner and from what I'd overheard through the gossip line Alice had really gotten some new techniques from a fancy school.

Next to Honey Comb Salon & Spa was the Buzz In and Out Diner owned by James Farley. Honey Springs's very first tattoo parlor, Odd Ink, was next to the diner. I wasn't sure who owned that. In fact, I didn't know any of the owners. It was all just idle gossip from Mae Belle and Bunny's morning coffee run that kept me in the know. They'd also said All About The Details, a new event center, was going in next to the tattoo place along with a bridal shop, Queen For The Day. Then there was me.

The Bean Hive.

The bait and tackle shop was the only shop that was on the pier. It was perfect for the tourists who wanted to fish for the day off the pier. They'd never closed like most of the past shops since the lake always had fishermen. This year was different.

The annual Honey Festival was also in a couple of days, hence the grand opening of the shops, and it did bring visitors far and wide to get a good sampling of our fine Kentucky honey and festival activities. This year the town council, of which my Aunt Maxi sits on the board, decided to move the festival from Central Park in downtown Honey Springs to the boardwalk. Vendors were going to be setting up along the boardwalk across from the shops. I was especially excited to purchase some fresh honey and honeycombs for the coffeehouse.

I'd yet to venture past my shop, but I did know there was some sort of clothing boutique, a knick-knack shop, a spa, a bar and at the very end was Crooked Cat Bookstore, which was an independent bookstore I'd spent many hours in during my summer visits. I fondly remembered a cat that snuggled up to me in the bean bag.

The smell of fresh coffee drifted out of the coffeehouse exactly how I'd envisioned it would. The warm scent filled me with joy where I wasn't sure I could have joy anymore.

When I opened the door to head back in, I smiled. The Bean Hive was a dream only a year ago and now a reality; I'd created it in my head and had worked hard to make the dream become real. After I filled my cup again, I walked back into the kitchen to check the casseroles I'd put in the oven for the afternoon lunch. I only cooked one thing a day for breakfast and lunch. I baked several things for the customers to enjoy and take home. The Bean Hive was a coffeehouse, not a restaurant, but we all know that food goes well with teas and coffee. It was my way of offering something for everyone.

Today's special was a sausage casserole that paired great with any flavor coffee or tea. Everything was made fresh, which made the coffeehouse fill with amazing, stomach rumbling aromas no one could refuse.

The bell over the door dinged. I rushed back in the dining area to greet the customer.

"I'm telling you something is wrong," Bunny Bowowski waddled into The Bean Hive with her brown pocketbook hung in the croak of her arm. "She didn't answer her phone all night last night."

"You know, I was by there just around eight o'clock and I did notice the strangest thing." Mae Belle Donovan stopped just inside the door and put her hand on Bunny's forearm. "You know those little plug-in candles that are in each one of her windows?"

"Do I?" Bunny rolled her eyes. "We downright got into a fight over them candles. In July of last year I told her that it was not Christmas and she needed to take them things down. In fact, it was hotter than a firecracker, not nary a thought of snow. She said it was decoration."

"Good morning, ladies." I greeted them like I'd done the past two mornings around this time.

According to Aunt Maxi, Bunny Bowowski and Mae Belle Donovan never left the house unless they were dressed in a dress, a shawl or coat (depending on the weather) and some sort of hat that sat on their heads like a bow as if it were completing the package.

They'd been friends for so long, they even resembled each other. Both had the exact same haircut, their grey hair was parted to the side and cut at chin length. They both carried a brown pocketbook that was perfectly held in the crook of their right elbow. Both were on the beautification committee. They came down every morning to get a look at the boardwalk to make sure everything was progressing right on schedule.

"Good morning to you." Bunny nodded and began to walk up to the counter. "Those are lovely daffodils."

"Thank you." I scooted them over to the right a little more so I could get a good view of my two customers. "Aren't they the most vibrant yellow you've ever seen?"

"Mmhmmm." Her brows formed a V.

"I got them at the farmer's market when I picked out my fresh produce and fruit. And this," I tapped the vase, very proud of my find, "I found this for one dollar at Wild and Whimsy."

"They do have some steals for an antique store." She rotated the clear hourglass vase that had a tin top and a round hole where the flowers went. She ran her finger along etched flowers in the glass. "You certainly got a bargain."

"Yes. I was very pleased." I pushed back a strand of my wavy black hair.

Wavy was a loose term for the springy naturally curly hair my head seemed to sprout as soon as water touched it. No matter how much I had it straightened, tried to straighten or even hide in a ponytail, a stray strand of hair sprung out from somewhere.

I glanced toward Mae Belle.

They weren't the spriest of women, but they certainly got around just fine.

"Hi do." Mae Belle gave a slight bow. "Something smells delicious."

"You are just in time for my country sausage casserole." I pointed to the glass pan I'd just taken out of the oven.

The melted cheese was still bubbling around the edges where it'd not cooled off yet.

"I'm letting it cool off so I can cut nice thick slices." I found it was best to let a dish cool for around ten minutes to not only set the casserole, but to let the flavors deepen and simmer within the ingredients. "If you'd like to have a cup of coffee while you wait for a slice of the casserole, I'd love to get you some."

"Oh, Roxanne, you do know us don't you." Bunny gave a theatrical wink. She pointed to one of the few café tables I had provided for the customers. "We'll go on over there."

I leaned way over the counter and whispered like I had a grand secret, "You can call me Roxy. All my friends do."

"Roxy with the amazing eyes." Bunny winked. "You do have beautiful blue eyes."

"Thank you." I smiled, grateful for the comment.

I poured two ceramic coffee mugs with The Bean Hive's own highlander grog and set them on a small round tray along with one of the silver cow cream pitchers I'd gotten on sale at Wild and Whimsy. Most of the china and silver I'd bought for The Bean Hive was from there, since the old things go great with the exposed brick walls, wood pallet furniture and big comfy chairs I'd used to decorate the shop, as well as the old tin signs and the chalkboard menus that hung above the counter.

"Roxy." A big smile curled up on her face. "Now that's a name with character."

"That's what I hear." I chuckled and excused myself where I retreated into the kitchen.

For the last year, I'd gotten up way before the rooster crowed, so to speak, which was about four a.m. around these parts. Only I hadn't been in these parts. Only recently had I moved back to Honey Springs. I'm not sure if it was to get away from the life I'd left behind due to my divorce or if I needed a little bit of familiarity or comfort. Regardless, I'm what I'd like to call a retired lawyer even at the young age of thirty. Retired because after my divorce, I hated lawyers. It was then that I'd listened to all that junk about following your passion. Doing what you love. Life is too short, yada-yada. One four a.m. morning, I couldn't sleep and fixed myself a cup of coffee. It was then and there that I decided I wanted to go to barista school and I've never looked back.

"The shops are looking great," I called over my shoulder on the way back to the kitchen to check the rest of the casseroles before I stuck the lunch ones in.

"We are pleased as peaches on how Cane Contractors has really stayed on schedule." I heard Bunny say after I walked through the door into the kitchen.

Cane Contractors. A lump formed in my throat at the sound of the name. It was very hard to swallow. I shook my head to make the thought go away.

"What on earth?" I looked at the convection oven with the morning sausage casseroles in it and noticed the digital buttons weren't lit up.

I hit the oven button and nothing. I opened the oven door. The casseroles were still running and lumpy. I stuck my hand in the oven and it was cold. Not a lick of heat.

"Great," I groaned and hurriedly took out a couple of the four casseroles I had in there and moved them to the other convection oven next to it where I crammed them in with the lunch quiches. "This is going to have to work." I gulped knowing it probably wasn't going to work since both of them required different cooking temperatures.

I headed back out to the shop and grabbed my cell phone out of the pocket of my apron and dialed my aunt Maxine.

"Aunt Maxi, I'm so glad you answered." My rapidly beating heart settled down after I'd heard the comforting sound of her voice.

"This better be good," the tone in her voice wasn't happiness. "I need my beauty sleep. I'm on the prowl ya know."

"Yeah, yeah." Prowl. My aunt was in her mid-sixties and widowed. Widowed at a young age too. But as far as I knew, she was happily single. "Listen, can you hurry down to the shop and grab some of the lunch quiches for me and put them in your oven to bake?" I asked.

"You didn't call a handyman yet?" She let me know that she'd warned me several times after I'd bought the place how the previous owner of the restaurant had undercooked food and eventually got shut down by the Health Department.

"No," I muttered, knowing I really should've listened to her but the cost was something I wasn't able to afford right now. "I was trying to wait until this first week was open and then I'd hire one."

"I'm going to say I told you so, just because I can say I told you so and you won't give no sass back. I told you so," she said in a playful voice. "I'll be right over."

"Thank you so much. I love you and I know you love me." A sigh of relief escaped me.

There weren't too many times Aunt Maxi didn't save me. In fact, the reason I'd come back to Honey Springs was due to her. I love my mom but she seemed to hover around me when I'd gone home to Lexington after my divorce. Aunt Maxi had lived in Honey Springs all her life and she was my dad's sister. Unfortunately, he'd died of cancer years ago. I'd spend summers here with Aunt Maxi and the cozy town had become a second home to me.

I loved the small shops scattered throughout the town. But the boardwalk and pier were my favorite spots in Honey Springs. Aunt Maxi owned a few rental properties, The Bean Hive being one as well as Crooked Cat Bookstore plus a couple residential places. Unfortunately for me, she didn't have any houses available, so I bought a pretty run-down cabin alongside the lake and only a four-minute bike ride from the coffeehouse.

It was a perfect place to live, but needed a few upgrades. Still, it was mine and I loved every part of it, even the broken ones.

"Are you ladies ready for your slice of country sausage casserole?" I asked and sliced into the warm casserole, plating two nice sized pieces on two lattice, milk glass plates. "Here you go." I set a plate down in front of each of them.

"This looks amazing, Roxy." Bunny leaned over the plate. She closed her eyes and inhaled. "And smells delicious."

There was nothing as satisfying to me as seeing someone who enjoyed something I'd made with my hands.

"Thank you." I took a step back and put my hands in a prayer position up in front of my face. "I'm honored. I hope you enjoy the taste too."

"I'm sure we will," she said.

Mae Belle didn't have to say anything. She'd already dug in and was on her third bite.

I walked over to the door not only to see if Aunt Maxi was on her way, but to see if there was anyone walking along the boardwalk who I could offer a free coffee to. Even if some of the construction workers were employed by Cane, there was a lot of construction going on and even they had to eat or at least warm up with a coffee. My eyes scanned the workers to make sure I didn't see anyone I knew from my past summers here. There was a bit of satisfaction and a bit of sadness when I didn't recognize any of them. It was probably a good thing.

"You've outdone yourself with this one," Mae Belle called from behind me and forced me to come back out of my memories that were good and bad.

"Thank you so much." I stared down the boardwalk where a tall, lean man with a yellow hardhat on was standing next to the new beauty salon and spa.

He had a set of plans rolled out in front of him. A couple of men on each side of him were looking at the plans. They nodded and spoke with each other. The early morning chill had yet to give way to the spring afternoon weather. I knew the spa was going to open along with most of the other shops before the annual spring Honey Festival in hopes that'd bring the tourists we needed to revitalize the sleepy town. That was one of the reasons I'd moved back. The fond memories of lazy days spent on the pier and watching all the people going in and out of the shops outweighed the only bad memory I'd had. Those days had been long gone and now I was going to do my part to help bring it back.

Not only did the Honey Springs economy need it, I needed it to help restore my soul.

"Are you two okay?" I asked on my way back to the counter.

They nodded and went back to discussing their friend who apparently hadn't shown up for a meeting or something.

I grabbed a thermos that could hold six cups of coffee and stuck it under the Bunn Industrial coffee maker to fill. While it filled up, I grabbed a few to-go cups. I ran a finger over the cute The Bean Hive logo I'd designed. It was fun to see the bee that had a coffee bean for a body come to life on the materials I'd had printed for merchandise as well as on marketing materials.

The bell over the door dinged and I looked up.

"Alexis Roarke," Bunny greeted the petite blonde. "We were just discussing where you've been."

"You have," Alexis Roarke wore her blond hair in a conservative nature with a bob cut just beneath her ears and straight across bangs. She had on pair of tennis shoes, khakis, and a pull over hoodie with the Honey Springs logo on it.

"I even went by your house and your *decorative* candles weren't even lit up." Mae Belle eyed her suspiciously.

"Why, Mae Belle Donovan," Alexis drew her hands up to her chest. "You do care about me."

"Of course, we do." Bunny pushed back the only extra chair at their café table. "Sit." She patted the seat. "Where have you been?"

Alexis waved her off and was content standing next to the table.

"I don't have time to sit. I've got to open the shop. Maxine Bloom is at it again," she said my aunt's name with exhaustion. "Raising the rent on the bookstore. I'm gonna have to stop volunteering at the Pet Palace."

"Why? Because you volunteer with Maxine?" Bunny asked and sipped on her coffee.

"No. So I can keep the bookstore open an extra day. I close early on Fridays so I can go volunteer. No more." She shook her head. She pointed at me and shook her finger. "I hear you are Maxine's niece."

"You hear right." I offered a warm smile in hopes she didn't hold it against me that my aunt Maxine was her landlord. "Did I also hear you say that you are the owner of Crooked Cat Bookstore?"

"I am." Her eyes narrowed as though she was sizing me up.

"I have fond memories of your bookstore when I used to come visit during the summer." A happy sigh escaped me. "I remember sitting in that big purple bean bag that was in the front window next to the cat tree. You had that little grey cat and that amazing banned book section."

"I'll be. I remember your eyes." A smile formed and reached her eyes. They twinkled as though the memory was bright. "That's when Maxine and I got along. She'd bring you in there while she was doing her property rounds and tell you to read books. I knew I was watching you."

"I believe my love of reading stems from you and all the time I spent in your store." I pointed to the coffee maker. "Can I get you a cup of coffee? On the house."

"Ours wasn't," Mae Belle grumbled under her breath.

"I'd love one to go. And give me one of them cake doughnuts." She pulled her chin to the side, and tilted her eyes over her shoulder as she enjoyed the look on Mae Belle's face.

With the to-go cup of coffee and The Bean Hive bag filled with a doughnut, she bid her friends goodbye.

"I'll see y'all at the town council meeting tomorrow. I've got a few things to say about this zoning thing and Maxine Bloom." She skirted out of the shop.

Mae Belle and Bunny put their heads together and both tried to whisper above the other. I figured it was a good time to take the workers the coffee.

"I'll be right back. I'm going to run some coffee down to the workers." I held the thermos up along with the cups.

The sun was popping up over the trees that stood along the lake like soldiers and filtered over the calm water of the lake. There were a couple of small bass boats running side-by-side with a couple of men in them, probably looking for a good inlet to bass fish.

The wood boards of the boardwalk groaned underneath each step I took as I got closer to the group of men.

"Good morning," I greeted them. "I'm Roxanne Bloom, owner of The Bean Hive." I gestured toward the coffee shop. "I've made all this coffee and only a few customers have come in." I left out the fact that I'd only had the same two customers all week long. "And I'd hate to see this fresh coffee go to waste, so I thought I'd bring it to y'all."

"That's mighty nice of you." The tall man grinned from under the hardhat. He kept his eyes on the thermos.

One of the men took the cups out of my hand while another one took the thermos.

"We appreciate that, don't we boys?" The man's deep voice echoed off the limestone banks of the lake. The glare of the sun reflecting off the lake made it difficult to see his face.

The men thanked me.

"If y'all get hungry, I also serve food." I smiled and clasped my hands in front of me. I was definitely trying to use the old saying that a way to a man's heart was through his stomach. Not that I was trying to get into any of their hearts, I wasn't, but I was trying to get to their stomachs and their wallets. "Enjoy."

"We will. And we will return your thermos," the man said before he went back to pointing out things about the spa.

It was my cue to head on back. They had work to do and so did I.

"Hello, honey." Aunt Maxi was leaning her bike up against the outside of the shop. She pulled off her knit cap. She tucked the hat in the purse that was strapped across her body and pulled out a can of hairspray. She raked her hand upward through her hair and used her other hand to spray it to high heaven. "You know, you need to get a bike rack."

"I do need a bike rack, but I also need to get a new oven or have this one looked at." I opened the door for her and let her walk in before me. "New hair color since yesterday?"

She gave the newly blond-colored hair another good spray before she stuck the can back in her purse and started toward the door.

"Alice Dee down at the Honey Comb says it's all the rage. Makes me feel young as a whippersnapper." She turned to me. The morning sun sprinkled down upon her.

I shook my head and realized having her bike up against the coffeehouse was probably not a good place for it to lean in case someone tripped over it.

Most of the community rode bikes everywhere since Honey Springs was a small, compact town that took pride in their landscape and Kentucky bluegrass that made the entire town look like a fancy landscape painting.

"You look a little like Phyllis Diller." And it wasn't just the hair. Aunt Maxi had put on a little too much makeup

"Well, well. If it's not Maxine Bloom." Bunny Bowowski didn't seem all that happy to see Aunt Maxi. "And with a new hairdo."

"You'll serve just about anybody." Aunt Maxi curled her nose at me.

"You two know each other?" I asked, hoping to bring a little peace between us.

"Know her?" Bunny scoffed. "She's been down at the Moose trying to get her claws into Floyd, my man."

"Don't flatter yourself, Bunny. I want a man that can walk without stopping every two feet so he can get his footing up under him so he don't fall." Aunt Maxi drew her chin in the air and looked down her nose. "Besides, that's not what's got you all worked up."

"Aunt Maxi is why I've come to Honey Springs." I patted my aunt on the back. "I used to come here when I was a child and spent many summers here. Right here in this very spot when it was the diner. I loved being here so much, that I decided to move here and open The Bean Hive."

I hoped that their mutual like for me would at least bring them together. The last thing I needed was my only two paying customers to boycott me because of Aunt Maxi.

"We will see you tomorrow, Roxy." Bunny stood up and motioned for Mae Belle to follow. "We've got committee stuff to do."

The three women gave each other the Baptist nod where they didn't wish ill-will but not necessarily success. The southern woman's way around good manners.

"Glad they're gone." Aunt Maxi spouted out and walked to the back of the shop. She put her hands on her hips and looked around. "This looks good," she said in approval. "Many customers?"

"Nope, you just ran off the only two I've had since I opened." I gave her a wry look. "Cup of coffee?"

"I can't. I've got to get your casseroles and head to a meeting. It's hard being a councilwoman." Aunt Maxi had held the office for over thirty years and was very proud of it. "That's why old Bunny is all mad. She and her group of cronies think that just because we are in craft group together that I'll just let them do whatever they want regarding the festivals and the beautification committee."

Apparently Aunt Maxi didn't agree on something in their meeting. Didn't surprise me. Aunt Maxi wasn't one to go along with the crowd when she was passionate about something. There were two things I knew not to get into with others: Politics and religion. Around here both were just as important as a new born baby, wedding, or a funeral. "They aren't too worried about whatever it is that you've made them mad about. They are worried about one of their friends."

"Who?" Aunt Maxi perked up and walked on my heels on our way back to the kitchen.

"I don't know. I can't remember her name. She actually came in." I grabbed the two lunch quiches I'd taken out of the oven earlier and wrapped them in tinfoil, pinching the sides as tight as I could. "She owns Crooked Cat."

"Alexis Roarke." Aunt Maxi groaned.

I laughed and stacked the two quiches. "She said that you two are fond of each other."

"Don't get me started on her because I don't come with brakes." Aunt Maxi picked up the quiches. "You know those left-over doughnuts you gave me yesterday?"

"Yes. What about them?" I asked.

"I took them to her last night. Sort of a peace offering," Aunt Maxi said. "She was just fine. So there's no need to worry about her. Those women love to worry. If they aren't gossiping or worried about someone, they're dead."

"They were happy to see her and that she was okay." I was just about to ask her about Alexis's claim that Aunt Maxi was going to raise the rent, but the bell over the shop door dinged, alerting me that someone had come in.

Aunt Maxi and I looked.

"Good morning, Maxine." The man I'd taken coffee to took off his hardhat with his left hand, his right gripped the thermos.

"Good to see you." Aunt Maxi's joy of seeing the man was evident all over her face. Even her eyes tipped up in the corners with giddiness.

"I wanted to thank you for the coffee. My men appreciate your kindness." His features were familiar. His big brown eyes were warm and matched the tender smile.

"I'm glad to see the two of you have mended ways. You know I believe everything happens for a reason." Aunt Maxi walked over to the door as she recited her favorite saying. "I'll have these back to you in a couple of hours. See you later, Patrick."

Patrick? I took a deeper look at the man standing in front of me. Patrick Cane? I looked a little deeper. Patrick Cane.

My heart sank

About the Author

For years, *USA Today* bestselling author Tonya Kappes has been self-publishing her numerous mystery and romance titles with unprecedented success. She is famous not only for her hilarious plotlines and quirky characters, but her tremendous marketing efforts that have earned her thousands of followers and a devoted street team of fans. Be sure to check out Tonya's website for upcoming events and news and to sign up for her newsletter! Tonyakappes.com

Also by Tonya Kappes

Olivia Davis Paranormal Mystery Series

SPLITSVILLE.COM

COLOR ME LOVE (novella)

COLOR ME A CRIME

Magical Cures Mystery Series

A CHARMING CRIME

A CHARMING CURE

A CHARMING POTION (novella)

A CHARMING WISH

A CHARMING SPELL

A CHARMING MAGIC

A CHARMING SECRET

A CHARMING CHRISTMAS (novella)

A CHARMING FATALITY

A CHARMING GHOST

A CHARMING HEX

A CHARMING VOODOO

Spies and Spells Mystery Series

SPIES AND SPELLS

BETTING OFF DEAD

GET WITCH OR DIE TRYING

A Laurel London Mystery Series

CHECKERED CRIME

CHECKERED PAST

CHECKERED THIEF

A Divorced Diva Beading Mystery Series

A BREAD OF DOUBT SHORT STORY

STRUNG OUT TO DIE

CRIMPED TO DEATH

A Ghostly Southern Mystery Series

A GHOSTLY UNDERTAKING

A GHOSTLY GRAVE

A GHOSTLY DEMISE

A GHOSTLY MURDER

A GHOSTLY REUNION

A GHOSTLY MORTALITY

A GHOSTLY SECRET

Kenni Lowry Mystery Series
FIXIN' TO DIE

Tonyakappes.com

Copyright

This book is a work of fiction. The characters, incidents, and dialogue are drawn from the author's imagination and are not to be construed as real. Any resemblance to actual events or persons, living or dead, is entirely coincidental.